"What do you want, Lily Garrett? Why are you here?"

"I'm applying for the job."

"You think you could handle it? Handle me?"

"That all depends on whether you're a gentleman or not."

He took another step, until his chest brushed her arm. "I'm not."

The cold air behind her and the heat in front met inside her, brewing up one hell of a storm. It wasn't enough he had that rugged cowboy thing going on, but he also oozed bad-boy sexy, which wasn't the least bit fair.

His hand lifted and he touched her hair. Just her hair. And she nearly dropped her soda. She needed to make her mouth work. For words to form. But that seemed way too difficult as his fingers brushed her cheek. "I don't think this is such a good idea."

"What?"

"You touching me."

"I'll stop if you want me to."

She closed her eyes. His thumb, callused and thick, followed the curve of her jaw all the way to her chin. "Stop." Her voice sounded weak, soft.

"You're old enough to know better," he whispered.

"Better than what?"

"That you shouldn't play with fire if you don't want to get burned."

Dear Reader,

Welcome to Trueblood, Texas!

Here's what I want to know—how come, when I
lived in Texas for five years, I never met a man
like Cole Bishop? That doesn't seem fair, does it? I
know there are men like Cole—rough and stern on the
outside, passionate and loving in private. I just haven't
met my Cole...yet.

Here's the other thing I want to know—how come
I can't be more like Lily Garrett? She's a pistol, that
Lily, and I do admire a woman who isn't afraid to
say what's on her mind.... Oh, wait. My friend (who's
reading over my shoulder) tells me I shouldn't lie to
my nice readers. I do say what's on my mind. In fact,
no one can stop me from sharing my two cents. That's
true, I guess, but Lily has such class, such flair, and
she's so darn quick! I usually think of the perfect
thing to say about two hours after the conversation
is over.

Here's what I know for sure—there's magic involved
in writing a novel. Oh, there's plot and character
and dialogue and all the usual stuff, but sometimes,
if I've been very, very good, the book will take wing
and soar, and all I have to do is hang on for the ride.
The Cowboy Wants a Baby was like that. It will
always have a special place in my heart, and I hope,
dear readers, that it will be a special book for you,
too.

I love to hear from readers! http://www.joleigh.com

Jo Leigh

TRUEBLOOD, TEXAS

The Cowboy Wants a Baby

Jo Leigh

HARLEQUIN®

TORONTO • NEW YORK • LONDON
AMSTERDAM • PARIS • SYDNEY • HAMBURG
STOCKHOLM • ATHENS • TOKYO • MILAN • MADRID
PRAGUE • WARSAW • BUDAPEST • AUCKLAND

Jo Leigh is acknowledged as the author of this work.

To my friends at Army Street with all my affection, and to Marsha for having such faith.

HARLEQUIN BOOKS
225 Duncan Mill Road, Don Mills,
Ontario, Canada M3B 3K9

ISBN 0-373-15336-8

THE COWBOY WANTS A BABY

Visit us at www.eHarlequin.com

Printed in U.S.A.

TRUEBLOOD, TEXAS

THE TRUEBLOOD LEGACY

THE YEAR WAS 1918, and the Great War in Europe still raged, but Esau Porter was heading home to Texas.

The young sergeant arrived at his parents' ranch northwest of San Antonio on a Sunday night, only the celebration didn't go off as planned. Most of the townsfolk of Carmelita had come out to welcome Esau home, but when they saw the sorry condition of the boy, they gave their respects quickly and left.

The fever got so bad so fast that Mrs. Porter hardly knew what to do. By Monday night, before the doctor from San Antonio made it into town, Esau was dead.

The Porter family grieved. How could their son have survived the German peril, only to burn up and die in his own bed? It wasn't much of a surprise when Mrs. Porter took to her bed on Wednesday. But it was a hell of a shock when half the residents of Carmelita came down with the horrible illness. House after house was hit by death, and all the townspeople could do was pray for salvation.

None came. By the end of the year, over one hundred souls had perished. The influenza virus took those in the prime of life, leaving behind an unprecedented number of orphans. And the virus knew no boundaries. By the time the threat had passed, more than thirty-seven million people had succumbed worldwide.

But in one house, there was still hope.

Isabella Trueblood had come to Carmelita in the late 1800s with her father, blacksmith Saul Trueblood, and her mother, Teresa Collier Trueblood. The family had traveled from Indiana, leaving their Quaker roots behind.

Young Isabella grew up to be an intelligent woman who had a gift for healing and storytelling. Her dreams centered on the boy next door, Foster Carter, the son of Chester and Grace.

Just before the bad times came in 1918, Foster asked Isabella to be his wife, and the future of the Carter spread was secured. It was a happy union, and the future looked bright for the young couple.

Two years later, not one of their relatives was alive. How the young couple had survived was a miracle. And during the epidemic, Isabella and Foster had taken in more than twenty-two orphaned children from all over the county. They fed them, clothed them, taught them as if they were blood kin.

Then Isabella became pregnant, but there were complications. Love for her handsome son, Josiah, born in 1920, wasn't enough to stop her from growing weaker by the day. Knowing she couldn't leave her husband to tend to all the children if she died, she set out to find families for each one of her orphaned charges.

And so the Trueblood Foundation was born. Named in memory of Isabella's parents, it would become famous all over Texas. Some of the orphaned children went to strangers, but many were reunited with their families. After reading notices in newspapers and church bulletins, aunts, uncles, cousins and grandparents rushed to Carmelita to find the young ones they'd given up for dead.

Toward the end of Isabella's life, she'd brought together more than thirty families, and not just her orphans. Many others, old and young, made their way to her doorstep, and Isabella turned no one away.

At her death, the town's name was changed to Trueblood, in her honor. For years to come, her simple grave was adorned with flowers on the anniversary of her death, grateful tokens of appreciation from the families she had brought together.

Isabella's son, Josiah, grew into a fine rancher and married Rebecca Montgomery in 1938. They had a daughter, Elizabeth Trueblood Carter, in 1940. Elizabeth married her neighbor William Garrett in 1965, and gave birth to twins Lily and Dylan in 1971, and daughter Ashley a few years later. Home was the Double G ranch, about ten miles from Trueblood proper, and the Garrett children grew up listening to stories of their famous great-grandmother, Isabella. Because they were Truebloods, they knew that they, too, had a sacred duty to carry on the tradition passed down to them: finding lost souls and reuniting loved ones.

PROLOGUE

THE YEAR WAS 1918, and the great war in Europe still raged, but Esau Porter was heading home to Texas.

The young sergeant arrived at his parents' ranch northwest of San Antonio on a Sunday night, only the celebration didn't go off as planned. Most of the townsfolk of Carmelita had come out to welcome Esau home, but when they saw the sorry condition of the boy, they gave their respects quickly and left.

The fever got so bad so fast that Mrs. Porter hardly knew what to do. By Monday night, before the doctor from San Antonio made it into town, Esau was dead.

The Porter family grieved. How could their son have survived the German peril, only to burn up and die in his own bed? It wasn't much of a surprise when Mrs. Porter took to her bed on Wednesday. But it was a hell of a shock when half the residents of Carmelita came down with the horrible illness. House after house was hit by death, and all the townspeople could do was pray for salvation.

None came. By the end of the year, over one hundred souls had perished. The influenza virus took those in the prime of life, leaving behind an unprecedented number of orphans. And the virus knew no boundaries. By the time the threat had passed, more than thirty-seven million people had succumbed worldwide.

But in one house, there still remained hope.

Isabella Trueblood had come to Carmelita in the late 1800s with her father, blacksmith Saul Trueblood, and her mother, Teresa Collier Trueblood. The family had traveled from Indiana, and left their Quaker roots behind.

Young Isabella grew up to be an intelligent woman who had a gift for healing and storytelling. Her dreams centered on the boy next door, Foster Carter, the son of Chester and Grace.

Just before the bad times came in 1918, Foster asked Isabella to be his wife, and the future of the Carter spread was secured. It was a happy union, and the future looked bright for the young couple.

Two years later, not one of their relatives was alive. How the young couple had survived was a miracle. And during the epidemic, Isabella and Foster had taken in more than twenty-two orphaned children from all over the county. They fed them, clothed them, taught them as if they were blood kin.

Then Isabella became pregnant, but there were complications. Love for her handsome son Josiah, born in 1920, wasn't enough to stop her from growing weaker by the day. Knowing she couldn't leave her husband to tend to all the children if she died, she set out to find families for each one of her orphaned charges.

And so the Trueblood Foundation was born. Named in memory of Isabella's parents, it would become famous all over Texas. Some of the orphaned children went to strangers, but many were reunited with their families. After reading notices in newspapers and church bulletins, aunts, uncles, cousins and grandparents rushed to Carmelita to find the young ones they'd given up for dead.

Toward the end of Isabella's life, she'd brought together more than thirty families, and not just her orphans. Many others, old and young, made their way to her doorstep, and Isabella turned no one away.

At her death, the town's name was changed to Trueblood, in her honor. For years to come, her simple grave was adorned with flowers on the anniversary of her death, grateful tokens of appreciation from the families she had brought together.

Isabella's son, Josiah, grew into a fine rancher and married Rebecca Montgomery in 1938. They had a daughter, Carrie Trueblood Carter, in 1940. Carrie married her neighbor William Garrett in 1965 and gave birth to Lily and Dylan in 1971, and daughter Ashley a few years later. Home was the Double G ranch, about ten miles from Trueblood proper, and the Garrett children grew up listening to stories of their famous great-grandmother Isabella. Because they were Truebloods, they knew that they, too, had a sacred duty to carry on the tradition passed down to them: finding lost souls and reuniting loved ones.

CHAPTER ONE

THE MANTEL OF the massive stone fireplace in the great room of the Double G ranch overflowed with calla lilies. The elegant white flowers had been placed with care just below the portrait of great-grandmother Isabella Trueblood, and Lily Garrett knew who was behind the sentimental gesture.

She turned to face her loved ones, and her gaze landed on her father, William. "I can't believe you did this, Daddy. You know they're my favorite. You're trying to make me cry, aren't you?"

"Nothing wrong with a tear now and again." With a smile that made him seem much younger than his sixty-one years, William leaned over and kissed her on the forehead. "There's nothing I wouldn't give you, darlin'," he whispered.

"I know, Daddy. Thank you." Before Lily let the moment disarm her further, she looked over at the couch. Her brother, Dylan, sat perched on the arm. "Hey, get over here. It's your birthday, too."

He shook his head. "I'm fine right where I am."

"You coward."

He shrugged. "That's me."

She sighed, even though she wasn't really upset. Dylan was shy about this kind of thing, which was peculiar, since he wasn't shy about anything else. But she didn't mind taking the spotlight for her twin.

"I'm only letting you off the hook because I'm so much older."

"Ha," he said. "By all of eight minutes."

"Quiet, you young whippersnapper." She smiled, really looking at him, appreciating him. He had the light-brown hair and blue eyes of their father, while Lily had inherited her mother's wavy black hair and green eyes, but they were well and truly twins. The bond between them... Well, sometimes even she didn't understand the connection.

Her gaze moved to the rest of the family. Her sister, Ashley, who looked disgustingly young and perky in her tennis whites. Six years Lily's junior, Ashley had taken time from her busy schedule at the ad agency to be at the birthday party.

Max was there, too. Although not related by blood, he was family in all the ways that were important. He'd grown up on the Double G, just as his father had before him. As ranch foreman, Max played a large part in making the horse and cattle ranch profitable. As a friend, he was even more important. Only five years older than Lily, he'd been a playmate, a tease, a strong shoulder to lean on.

"So are you going to open the presents or what?" Ashley checked her watch impatiently. "I've got a game at four."

"Your game can wait." William walked over to the big leather couch and eased down, a contented sigh escaping the moment he was off his feet. "It's not often we have the two of them home on this special occasion."

"They're going to live here forever now," Ashley said. "We'll have hundreds more birthdays to celebrate."

"But none like this." Lily took Ashley's arm and maneuvered her to the couch, next to their father.

Now that she had everyone's attention, Lily cleared her throat. "This isn't an ordinary day. Aside from it being our thirtieth birthday—which, by the way, I feel is totally unbelievable since I don't feel twenty-five, let alone thirty—today marks a new beginning for me."

Her brother's right brow arched in a silent question.

"You've all had to put up with a lot from me for the last seven months. I want you to know that I appreciate your patience and your generosity."

Ashley's eyes widened. "*You* appreciate *us?* It's a rare day indeed."

"Hush, Ashley, and let me finish." Lily moved to the center of the room and glanced up at the second floor for a moment. She cleared her throat, then went on with the speech she'd prepared that morning. "The construction on the new offices is nearing completion, which should be a relief to everyone."

Ashley clapped, prompting Lily into giving her younger sibling one of her better glares.

"Finders Keepers is well on its way to becoming the success we knew it would be," Lily went on. "There's a need for what we're doing. Too many people are lost and lonely, longing for what we have in abundance in this very room. It's a cold world out there without someone who loves you. Someone to love. And it's part of our legacy to help." She hesitated, wondering if she had the nerve to say the rest. But then she looked into her father's eyes.

"I also want to let you guys know that as of this day, I won't be griping about Jason Gill anymore. In fact, I won't even bring up his name."

Ashley's phony choking earned her a pinch from Dylan. Lily didn't let the episode shake her.

"I'm finished with that," she continued. "My entire focus is going to be on the agency and nothing else. But I will say one last thing. I know there's a lesson in this. There's a reason I fell for the rotten son of a bitch, and a reason I didn't know he was married. Unfortunately, I have no clue what that reason is. But I figure if it wasn't for endings, there wouldn't be new beginnings, right?"

Tears came to her eyes, but she blinked them back. The speech, the sentiment, were totally unlike her. She prided herself on her no-nonsense approach to life. Maybe it was turning thirty. Maybe it was the heat. She had no idea what had prompted her to get all mushy. But enough of that. She pushed her shoulders back, took a deep cleansing breath, then made the mistake of looking at Dylan.

His eyes seemed focused on something far away. She had a good idea what he was thinking about. Last year had been tough for him, too. He'd lost a part of himself while he'd been in Dallas. She wished with all her heart that she could take away his pain as well as her own. At least they were home, where they could rebuild their lives and find some peace.

"This is what's important," she said, mostly to Dylan, but to herself as well. "Being here with the people we love, and who love us. That's the best present of all."

"Uh, Lily?"

She was almost afraid to respond. "Yes, Ashley?"

"Does that mean you won't be wanting the sweater I got you?"

Laughter shifted the mood, and when Lily walked

over to strangle her little sister, things got even live-lier. Although she didn't hurt Ashley, she did pluck her gift from the pile on the coffee table. ''Sweater, eh?''

Nearly tearing off the white bandage on her hand, a reminder not to save feral puppies without thick gloves, Lily ripped into the purple-and-white package that Ashley most assuredly had paid someone to wrap. Lily flipped open the box underneath. But there was no sweater. Instead, she pulled out a Sherlock Holmes hat, a meerschaum pipe, and a magnifying glass.

Dylan cracked up and Ashley's cheeks turned pink.

''This is so cool!'' Lily plopped the hat on her head and stuck the pipe in her mouth, then turned to her brother. ''Watson, bring me my violin.''

Dylan got up off his perch on the side of the couch and approached her, a sly smile tugging the corners of his mouth. ''Watson?'' He swiped the hat from her head. ''I don't think so.''

She reached to grab it, but Dylan held it too high. ''Give that back. It's mine!''

''Finders keepers,'' he said, dangling the woolen cap tauntingly in front of her.

''I've got your finders keepers right here, buddy.'' She jumped for the hat and caught the bill. They tugged back and forth, causing much hooting and laughter from Ashley and Max, until, at William's urging, Dylan gave up. Lily put the hat on, grinning at her victory. They hadn't tussled in years. It re-minded her of their childhood. There had been lots of roughhousing, but very little ill will. Well, except for the time he'd broken into her diary. But since that had happened fifteen years ago, she might be ready to forgive him.

"It's my turn," Dylan said, taking the second of the purple-and-white packages. He, unlike Lily, took his time opening the gift. First the ribbon, then each piece of tape. It was maddening. Finally, though, he hit a box. He opened it and grinned as he pulled out a mahogany door plaque that read Finders Keepers in beautiful gold script.

"For the new office," Ashley said.

"It's a knockout, Ash." Dylan passed the plaque to Lily, then kissed his little sister on the cheek. "You did good."

"Was there any doubt?"

Lily didn't respond. She was too busy admiring the beautiful workmanship on the plaque. The investigative agency was as real as the wood in her hands. Their intervention had brought three couples together and reunited two mothers and their children—everything Dylan and she had talked about when they'd decided to carry on the Trueblood legacy.

She couldn't wait until the offices were finished. Maybe she'd even open a bottle of champagne when they put this plaque on the door.

Max cleared his throat, getting her attention. He nodded at the other presents on the table. She plucked a pink bag from the pile and read the card first. It was from her father, and the message was as sweet and corny as he was. Inside she found a jewelry box.

She could sense, even before opening the lid, that she needed to sit down for this one. She settled on the couch, forcing Ashley to squeeze against the arm. When she opened the box, her heart stopped. She recognized the necklace instantly. It had been her mother's.

"We thought you ought to have that when you turned thirty." William squeezed her hand. "She'd be so proud of you."

Lily lifted the elegant teardrop diamond on the slim gold chain. She'd seen her mother wear this on the most special of occasions. It had been her pride and joy. "Help me?" she asked, turning her back to her father and lifting her hair. His fingers trembled slightly as he struggled with the catch, but she didn't mind the wait. It gave her time to settle her own emotions. She still missed her mother so much.

"There you go, darlin'."

She let her hair loose and rose to look in the hallway mirror. The diamond hung beautifully on her neck, just below the hollow. It was stunning, but the importance wasn't in the perfect three-carat stone. It was in the memories. And in the future. She'd give her daughter the necklace, and with it, all the stories of Lily's mother, and her mother before her.... All the proud heritage of the Truebloods, who'd risen from the ashes of the worst epidemic the world had ever known, only to plunge into the work of reuniting families, finding lost loved ones, creating hope from despair.

"Come back, Lily. Dylan's opening the next one!"

She left the mirror, but not before she said a silent thanks to her mother.

Dylan had nearly finished his painstaking unwrapping by the time she sat back down on the couch. He got a jewelry box, too. Her father's watch. The one William had been given by the Ranchers' Association. The one he'd worn each time their mother had donned the necklace.

"Dad, I—"

"It's your time, son. I'm just glad I'm here to see you wear it."

Dylan didn't speak. He took off his own battered watch and put on the heavy silver timepiece. It looked right on his arm. As if it had always been there.

"There's only two more," Ashley said impatiently. "So, would you guys please open them together? And, Dylan, I swear to God, if you don't rip the paper like a normal human being, I'll whack you with my racket."

"You try, little sister, and you won't sit down for a week."

"Why? You'd take away the chairs?"

"Very amusing." Dylan stood tall, reaching his full six-feet-one-inch and folding his muscular arms across his chest. "Amusing, and yet highly annoying."

"Just open the damn present."

"Ashley, language."

"Sorry, Dad."

Lily interceded by grabbing the next gift. Inside the bag was the most beautiful journal. It had her name inscribed on the outside, and inside was page after crisp white page, just ready for her favorite purple pen and her most private thoughts. "Max."

He nodded. "I remember you saying you were reaching the end of your last one."

"Handsome *and* smart. What a combination."

He blushed, which had been her intention, and she stood to give him a thank-you kiss on the cheek. But as she turned, her attention was diverted. Sebastian

Cooper stood in the doorway, his face ashen and his eyes dark and terrible. She hadn't seen him much since his wife had disappeared. He looked like he'd been chewed up and spit out.

She got Dylan's attention and motioned toward the door. She heard a small gasp as he turned to see his best friend. Which meant Sebastian's condition had worsened very recently.

Dylan rushed around the couch and reached Sebastian's side at the same time Lily did.

"What is it?" Dylan's hands formed fists, something he'd done his whole life when he was terribly scared.

"I'm sorry. I should have called."

"What's wrong? Is it Julie?"

Sebastian shook his head. "It's not that. Or maybe it is, I don't know. All I'm sure of is the San Antonio cops couldn't find the River Walk without a guide. It's been seven months—"

Lily winced at his obvious pain. It must be torture. Julie had vanished early in January, the apparent victim of a car-jacking. So far the police had no leads, and Dylan had only been able to do so much investigating without tipping his hand. He hadn't wanted to push his services on Sebastian, but it had been impossible for him to sit by and do nothing. Julie and Sebastian meant too much to him.

When Lily had asked Dylan why he didn't just insist on heading the case, he'd talked to her about friendship and loyalty and male pride. She hadn't completely understood, but he remained adamant that before he could pull out all the stops, Sebastian needed to ask for his help.

It appeared he just had.

DYLAN GOT OUT the Johnnie Walker Black and poured Sebastian two fingers. The family had dispersed until dinner, so Dylan joined his friend at the kitchen table, handing him the glass. "Tell me what you know." Dylan probably knew as much as Sebastian did about the case, but he had the feeling his friend needed to talk about it.

Sebastian's hand shook as he held the amber liquid. "The only evidence they found was some blood on the back seat of the car. Julie's blood."

Dylan made sure he didn't react at all to the bald words. At least not outwardly. Sebastian needed him to be strong now. But it was damn hard.

Julie and Sebastian meant more to him than anyone outside his family. Hell, he'd grown up with Sebastian, the two of them riding the rodeo circuit all through high school. They'd even gone to college together, and that's when Julie had entered the picture. Beautiful Julie. Who had called him her white knight, but married Sebastian. Dylan couldn't bear to think of her hurt, or worse.

"They traced the last few hours before her disappearance. She'd been to the bank—to the safe deposit box."

"What did she do there?"

Sebastian shrugged. "Not much. Got some papers, I think. But someone must have seen her there. Assumed she'd gotten valuables."

"And followed her."

Sebastian knocked back his drink, shuddering as the scotch went down. "Followed her and took her." He stared at Dylan, his eyes filled with more pain than any man should have. "The nights are the worst. I can't sleep. I keep thinking about what she's going through."

"We'll find her, Sebastian. I swear on my life, we'll find her."

"I kept thinking the police would find her. That it had to be something simple, a misunderstanding, that she'd left because I'd said something thoughtless, but she would have called. She isn't cruel. Dammit, I should have come to you first."

"It's good that the police are involved. But they have too many other cases. I swear to you, Sebastian, I'll find her."

Sebastian nodded. "I know." He swallowed hard, then tried to smile. "Remember Christmas?"

"Of course."

"She was so happy about the locket. So thrilled that I'd had the stones replaced."

"It meant a lot to her."

Sebastian leaned across the big oak dining table. "I keep thinking that's what the bastard saw. That the necklace drew his attention. If I hadn't given it to her—"

"Stop it. You didn't do this. It's not your fault."

"How do you know?"

"I know this—when she gets back, she's going to need you. If you rake yourself over the coals like this, you won't be any good for her."

He leaned back, nodding. "Right. I need to be strong for her."

"Let the detective in charge know you've hired us. I'll need to see their reports."

"I will."

Dylan nodded at the scotch bottle. "Need another?"

"Yeah. But I'm not going to. If I start drinking now, I don't think I'll be able to stop."

"Right. So why don't you kick back. Take a swim or something. We're having dinner in a couple of hours."

"I can't, Dylan. I wish I could."

"You don't have to see anyone. I could arrange that."

Sebastian stood. "I have to go. I'm grateful to you, buddy. And listen." He swallowed again, his Adam's apple too visible. He'd lost weight. "Whatever happens—"

"We'll find her."

Sebastian turned away. A lock of his hair fell over his eye. Julie would have pushed it back, then she would have kissed him. It was something she did without fail. She'd been a sucker for Sebastian since day one. Dylan was glad she'd found happiness. Now all he had to do was bring her back to the arms of the man she loved.

Failing wasn't an option.

LILY RAISED her soda glass. "To us."

The rest of the family joined her in the impromptu toast. "To us."

They drank their assorted beverages and went on with the birthday dinner. Max and her father were already deep in discussion about the new paddock. Ashley, still in her tennis outfit, ate as if calories didn't exist. Dylan hardly touched his food.

She knew Julie's kidnapping weighed heavily on him—even more so now that he'd agreed to take the case. She wondered again if Dylan knew he was still in love with Julie. It had broken his heart when she married Sebastian, but good old Dylan hadn't said a word. He'd just stood there as best man and watched his one true love marry his closest friend.

So much of what had happened to Dylan was connected to that moment. His decision to leave San Antonio and work for the Dallas P.D. His undercover work infiltrating J. B. Crowe's mob family. The fateful error that had blown his cover.

Most people wouldn't tie all those events together, but most people didn't know Dylan the way she did. Sometimes—she wouldn't swear on a bible or anything—but sometimes she felt absolutely sure that she could read his mind. And that he could read hers. More than that, she felt his pain. Not to the degree he felt it, but it was there. A dull ache that told her Dylan was in trouble. It didn't seem to matter how far away he was, she always knew.

The ache was strong tonight. She wasn't at all sure he should have taken the case. If he failed…

And even if he didn't, the outcome was probably going to devastate him. The odds of Julie being alive after seven months were slim.

Dylan shoved some food around on his plate. She reached over and touched his hand. Startled, he looked at her.

"It's going to be okay," she whispered.

"I don't know."

"I do. Because you're going to do everything possible. You're the best man for the job and there's not going to be one stone left unturned. If anyone on earth can find her, it's you."

He nodded slowly, unconvinced, she thought.

"Little brother."

The appellation always made him smile. Eight

minutes didn't make him her "little" anything. But his smile failed to appear this time.

"Dylan, I know it's hard, but for Dad's sake, try. Eat something, just a little. Smile, even if you don't mean it."

He sighed. "I am pretty good at appearing to be something I'm not. And right now that means being in the mood to celebrate."

"After dinner, why don't we sit down and talk about what we know so far, and what's next."

He smiled, and damned if she didn't believe the transformation. "Good idea, Lily." He ate some steak, drank some iced tea, laughed at something Ashley said.

But the ache was still heavy in Lily's chest. The ache that told her Dylan was dying inside.

CHAPTER TWO

LILY'S FIRST VIEW of Eve Bishop's mansion came after almost a mile of winding road, flanked on each side with huge chinquapin oaks she'd give a pretty penny to see in the fall. The trees cast shimmering shadows on the road and her car in a windblown ballet.

The house itself was equally awe inspiring. Two-story Victorian, it was registered with the historic society as one of the original German mansions built in the late 1800s. As she drove closer, Lily could see the facade wasn't quite up to snuff. It needed paint and the garden was overgrown. But then Eve was in her seventies, and Lily had grown increasingly alarmed over the woman's frail health.

She'd met Eve while volunteering for the Texas Fund for Children, a large charitable organization that provided funding for a children's hospital and rehabilitative center, staff for the two largest orphanages in the state and many other educational and health programs. The whole shebang had been started by Eve and her late husband, and Eve had worked hands-on to build the foundation for over twenty years.

Lily parked the car in the circular drive and stepped out into the brutal July sun. With a high in the hundreds and the air thick with humidity, it wasn't a pleasant place to dawdle. But she did. She lingered in the garden for a moment, her mind's eye seeing what the grounds were meant to be when tended properly.

At the massive front door, she hesitated once more. Eve had asked her to come by, but had been quite mysterious about her reasons. Lily hoped it wasn't because she was ill. Aside from admiring Eve for her philanthropy, she liked the woman very much and considered her a real friend.

She rang the doorbell, hearing its echo inside, then waited. The house was so large, easily ten thousand square feet, that unless Eve had help, it was going to take her a while to get to the door. To Lily's surprise it was opened almost immediately by a young woman with a welcoming smile.

"I'm Lily Garrett. Here to see Eve."

"She's expecting you," the woman said as she pulled the door open further. She was in her twenties, Lily guessed, and of Hispanic heritage. Her dark hair had been pinned up, and she wore shorts and a T-shirt, completing the ensemble with bare feet.

"Please, come this way." Her accent was slight, lilting. She led Lily through the broad foyer, her bare soles slapping the white marble floor, then stopped at a door just a few feet down the hallway. She knocked twice but didn't wait for a response. Lily nodded her thanks as she stepped inside.

The room captivated her instantly. Very Victorian in style, decorated in different hues of pink and white, it was made perfect by the elegant tea cart holding a silver service. Eve sat on an overstuffed chair, her petite body dwarfed by the chair's velvet wings.

"Lily. I've made tea."

"I see. It looks wonderful."

Eve patted the cushion of the love seat next to her chair. "Come. And tell me if you prefer milk or lemon."

"Milk, I think."

For the next few moments, Eve went through the slow ritual of afternoon tea, complete with tiny crustless watercress sandwiches, pink petits fours with icing that matched the color of the walls exactly, and little lumps of sugar doled out with silver tongs.

Lily took advantage of the lull to study the decor. Lush bouquets of fresh flowers were on the mantel and an end table. A white upright piano was the centerpiece of the far wall, and a brick fireplace flanked by bookshelves did the honors on the wall to her left. Antique dolls stared wide-eyed from various perches throughout the room, their bright curls adding a bit of life to the old-fashioned library.

Above the fireplace was a portrait, and Lily knew instantly that it was of Eve. She'd been much younger then, her now silver curls a deep coppery red. Her skin was smooth, her long neck arched and coy. The artist had captured her spirit, especially in her eyes. But the vivid blue in the picture had faded on the older woman.

Eve handed Lily a plate and a teacup, waited for her to take a sip, then sighed.

"What is it, Eve? Is something wrong?"

The old woman's hand trembled as she put her cup on the tea cart. "Several things, in fact."

"Is there something I can do?"

"I dearly hope so."

Lily took another sip of tea, but she hardly tasted it, her curiosity was so great.

"The simple fact is that I'm dying."

Lily nearly dropped her cup at the stark words. "Oh, no. Please, not that."

Eve nodded. "I don't mind very much. Honestly. I've had a rich and full life. My days now are mostly about pain, feeling it, treating it, ignoring it. My hands have become traitors and my eyes, well, maybe it's not so terrible to see the world in shadow."

"Is it really that bad?"

"Sometimes. But nothing hurts as much as the heaviness in my heart. And that's why I've called you."

"How can I help?"

Eve leaned back in her chair as if the effort of sitting upright had become too much for her. "I have a grandson."

"You've never mentioned him."

"I haven't. Because I haven't seen him in five years. I haven't spoken to him or heard about him. My son, his father, died four months ago. He had a heart attack. He hadn't spoken to Cole in five years, either."

"Why?"

"That's not important," she said, her brow furrowed with the effort of the conversation. "What is important is that I see my grandson before I die. I won't be able to rest until I do. Can you understand?"

"Of course. You love him."

"More than he'll ever know."

"Do you know where he lives?"

She shook her head slowly. "The last I heard, he was in Houston. But that probably isn't where he is now."

"Do you have any idea what he does?"

"No. Business, perhaps ranching. I don't know."

"I see."

"You don't. But you don't have to. Lily, I trust you. I know you'll bring him back. I'll pay twice your normal fee if you'll abandon all other cases to concentrate on this one."

"You don't have to do that."

"I don't have to do anything. But I'm a rich old woman whose shopping sprees are over."

Lily had no intention of arguing with her. She'd send an appropriate bill when the job was done. If, in fact, it ended satisfactorily. "I'd like to take this job, Eve, but I have to make something clear. I won't bring him back against his will. We reunite families that want to be reunited."

"Fine. Then I'll trust you to make him want to come home."

"Fair enough. I'll do my best."

"I know that, Lily. That's why I called you. I've done a little research of my own. I'm impressed with this new company of yours. But believe me when I say it was only because I'd met you and seen how you operate that I considered hiring you. Finding my grandson is the most important thing in my life. And that life, if one believes the doctors, will end in approximately six months."

"Please don't say that. Anything can happen. Miracles."

Eve's smile changed her face. The beauty of the portrait was still there despite the ravagement of years. "There are no miracles. Only things to regret. I don't want to go that way, you see. I don't want to die with this terrible regret."

"I do understand, Eve. I do."

Eve's pale-blue gaze met Lily's and held it steady.

The determination there was like steel. "Find him. Do whatever you have to do to bring him home. He's my only heir. He'll inherit it all. Make sure he understands that."

Lily nodded.

"Now drink your tea. It's probably cold by now."

MAX SANTANA yearned for a shower. A long, cold one. Riding out to the far pasture hadn't bothered him, but hauling that big mother cow out of a muddy bog had worn him to the bone. It was the heat. Normally San Antonio was in the high eighties this time in July. But a heat wave had settled across the state, shooting the temperature and the humidity to record levels.

He loved everything about this place except the high heat. Days like this, he had to keep his mind occupied on cool things. Iced tea. Snow. A long swim in a chilly pool.

The only thing Max wanted more than a dip in the pool was a woman.

As he rounded the corner of the big house, he bumped into something soft and sweet. Lily.

"Hey, Max."

"Sorry about that."

She waved the small accident away.

Lily was a woman all right, but to him she was practically a sister. What he needed was a stranger with loose morals. Yes, indeed. But he'd think about that in the shower. "Dylan's looking for you."

"Pardon?"

"You know. Your brother. He's looking for you."

"I've been out." She sounded distracted, her voice was softer than normal. And she hadn't smiled once.

"What's wrong?"

She didn't answer him.

"It's not that son of a bitch Jason Gill, is it? 'Cause I know where he lives and I've got vacation time coming."

"No, no. It's nothing like that."

He folded his arms across his chest and frowned at her. He wanted to look down his nose at her, but with her being five foot nine and him six-one, his scowl wasn't nearly as effective as it should have been. The more he studied her, the more he knew something was wrong. Lily had her hair up in some sort of tortoise-shell contraption, but a long strand had escaped captivity and hung down past the middle of her back. Lily didn't miss things like that unless she was pre-occupied or worried.

"Max, calm down. It's a new case, that's all."

"What kind of case?"

"I need to find a missing heir."

He grinned. "How much is at stake? I could sure use an inheritance."

"You could, huh? And what would you do with your millions, Mr. Santana?"

"I'd buy the O'Neill place."

She smiled, finally. "You are the most predictable man. So why don't you tell me where my little brother is?"

"He's in the office, and I'm going to tell him you called him that."

"You do, and I'll tell that O'Neill girl you've got the hots for her." The O'Neill girl was about fifty, and ornery as hell.

"Lily, don't threaten me. You know I can be vindictive as hell."

She slugged him in the shoulder, and for a skinny girl like her, she made it hurt. "You don't have a vindictive bone in your body. But you sure need a shower." She waved her hand in front of her nose and made a face at him. "You smell like wet cow."

He grunted, then headed off again. After his shower, he'd dive in the pool so fast he'd hardly feel the splash. Oh, yeah.

DYLAN WAS IN the makeshift office, actually a spare bedroom in the old part of the house. They'd moved in two desks and a filing cabinet, then loaded the place with electronic equipment: fax, computers, printers, phones, scanner, all of which would be transferred to the upstairs offices as soon as they were ready. For an interim space, the bedroom wasn't bad. Just small.

Lily put her purse in her bottom drawer then waited while Dylan finished his phone call. From his tone, she gathered it was business, and as she shamelessly eavesdropped, she realized he was talking to Bill Richardson, one of the homicide detectives working on Julie Cooper's case.

Searching for Cole Bishop was going to prevent her from assisting Dylan, but given the circumstances, it couldn't be helped. With Eve so ill, there wasn't a moment to waste. Besides, Dylan on his own was quite formidable, and she had no doubt that he'd do everything possible to find Julie. She just hoped he wouldn't get hurt. Either physically or emotionally. So much was at stake.

"I'll get back to you," Dylan said as he acknowledged her with a nod. "And see what you can do about those files, huh?" He listened for another few moments, said his goodbye and hung up. His attention was focused on her now, but she could see the strain of the morning's work on his face.

"How goes it?"

He shrugged. "Just trying to get up to speed. What was your meeting about?"

"I've got a case."

"Now?"

She nodded. "I'm sorry. I know how important it is to concentrate on finding Julie, but this is something of an emergency." She explained about Eve's request, and about the ticking clock. Dylan had met Eve on several occasions and his concern for her was immediate.

"Okay, I can do this on my own, but I think we need to get an assistant now instead of waiting for the offices to be finished."

"I agree. Any suggestions?"

He shook his head. "I'll make some calls in the morning."

Lily turned on her computer, ready to start the search for Cole Bishop. She heard Dylan curse softly, and when she looked up, he was staring at his notepad, his face a mask of frustration.

"What's wrong?"

He shook his head. "Things aren't adding up right."

"What do you mean?"

"Nothing concrete. It's more gut feeling than anything else. Something's eating at me."

"Well, then, you'd better pay attention. I don't know anyone who has better gut instincts than you."

He gave her a sardonic grin. "Not always."

She hadn't meant for the conversation to go there.

Dylan had been on an undercover assignment in Dallas the previous year. His gut instincts had taken him into the very heart of J. B. Crowe's mob family, but last October, he'd made one mistake—and that was all it took in his line of work. His cover had been blown, and he barely made it out of there alive. "Come on, Dylan. Did we or didn't we agree not to wallow in the past?"

"We agreed. But as I recall, it was after you ate an entire pint of Ben & Jerry's as you rehashed some memories I'm too much of a gentleman to bring up."

"Subtle. Like a sledgehammer."

"All I'm saying is the things we went through are a part of us. I don't think we can forget about them."

"But we don't have to beat ourselves up over and over, do we? Frankly, I don't want to live like that."

He leaned back in his chair and linked his hands behind his neck. "So why don't you find someone new? Someone who isn't married?"

"Date? Me? No. No way."

"Why not? You planning on becoming a nun?"

"Knock it off. Of course not. But I'm certainly not going to get myself involved this soon after— I mean, anything I would do now would be a rebound thing, right? I don't trust rebound things."

"Yeah, I suppose. But that doesn't mean you can't go out. There's such a thing as dating for fun."

"Which you would know about how?"

"Point taken."

"I think, for us, for now, we need to focus on the agency. In a year or so, we can rethink things, but now? Let's just be detectives."

"Right. Good answer."

She sighed. "So quit bugging me. I have work to do."

He didn't say anything, but about two minutes later, a rubber band hit her in the shoulder. Being so much older and more mature than Dylan, she let it pass.

WHEN LILY LEFT the office, it was almost eight. Dylan was hungry—he hadn't eaten since noon—but the idea of joining the family for dinner didn't sit well. He didn't want to make small talk, and he certainly didn't want to discuss his progress on the case.

Progress. As if he'd made any. The police were cooperating, to a degree, but that was only because he'd been part of the brotherhood. The evidence was sketchy as hell. Would car-jackers be sophisticated enough to wear gloves? Why else would there be no fingerprints in the car? Did they simply hold a gun to her head and force her out? Then why was there blood on the back seat?

It didn't make sense, and Dylan's instinct told him it wasn't a car-jacking. And yet, there was no ransom note. No demands. There had to be something else, some third possibility he couldn't see yet. She could have taken off, of course, but that wasn't Julie's style. He'd just keep digging until he figured it out.

His gaze shifted to a framed photograph on the wall behind the credenza. In it, he was with Julie and Sebastian, all smiles. Sebastian's arm was around Julie's waist and Julie's head rested on his shoulder. They were the picture of connubial bliss. Although they'd spent the day on the ranch, they'd been AWOL for about an hour after lunch, and Dylan knew exactly what they'd been doing.

He'd tried like hell not to let his imagination run wild, but he should have known better. With Julie, he had no willpower, no control. She came to him in dreams, while he was out riding, during business meetings. He'd thought by now he would have accepted that she'd chosen Sebastian. He'd been wrong.

He opened his bottom drawer and took out the bottle of aged scotch he kept there. But he didn't pour any. Instead, his gaze moved back to the photograph. To the necklace Julie wore with such pride. It was a silver heart that opened to reveal a small picture of the happy couple. It had been her mother's locket and Sebastian had scored major points for fixing it up like he had.

Dylan had given her earrings. But she wasn't wearing those in the photo. Just the necklace. Which was appropriate, of course. But he'd wished...

Screw that. It was over. Over and done, and Julie was with Sebastian. If Julie was alive, that is. If he could find her.

Although he wasn't a man who ordinarily prayed, he closed his eyes and repeated the desperate bargain that had become almost a mantra in the last six months. "God, please keep her safe. Bring her home. If you do that, I swear I'll stop loving her."

CHAPTER THREE

LILY TURNED UP the music as she merged onto U.S. 87. Another few hours and she'd reach Abilene. She'd found Cole Bishop easily enough. Now came the hard part. Getting him to come back with her.

Thanks to the Internet, she'd actually learned a good deal about his work. He had a successful mid-size ranch—the Circle B—just outside the small city of Jessup where he raised prize-winning Black Angus cattle. He had an excellent breeding program, but what he was most noted for was the way he managed the ranch. His techniques had been written up in *The Cattlemen* and the *High Plains Journal,* two big trade magazines. His approach to ranching was modern and cost-effective. Clearly, he was a smart cookie.

What she didn't find was anything about the man himself. No personal information at all. She couldn't find any pictures, either.

It occurred to her that perhaps Mr. Bishop wanted to connect with Eve again, but that he didn't know how. Men, especially ranchers, could be stubborn as mules. So maybe her appearance would be just the excuse he needed to mend his fences and go back into the fold.

But somehow she doubted it. Why? She couldn't say. Like her brother, she trusted her gut instincts. They'd always been alike that way. Most of her insights had been about Dylan; it was a twin thing, which she'd discovered wasn't uncommon at all. But when she'd moved out of the house, other events seemed to trigger that sixth sense of hers. It wasn't as if she had ESP or anything. Just that from time to time her radar would go off.

It had gone off with Jason Gill, but she'd ignored it. There had been that small worried voice in the back of her head when he'd asked her to leave New York and transfer to the Dallas office. But had she listened? Oh, no. She'd moved, lock, stock and barrel. Once she'd turned off her receiver, it had stayed off. She'd believed every honeyed lie, and she'd fallen hard. She still got monthly issues of *Bride* magazine at the house. Instead of canceling the damn subscription, she preferred to stack the magazines in a pile by her bed. A towering reminder to heed her intuition.

Of course, sometimes listening to the quiet voice inside led to things that were hard to deal with. As a forensics specialist working for the FBI, she'd learned how to go by the book. Except that one time. The small voice had led her to discover that the death of a pregnant teenager and the child inside her had not occurred in a drive-by shooting, as the police believed, but at the hands of her own father.

She'd realized then that forensics wasn't where she belonged. It wasn't all bad. But the case of the teenager, and of course the whole Jason mess, convinced her to leave Dallas and come home. That, at least, had been a positive thing.

The memories had shattered her good mood, and that wasn't acceptable. She turned up the radio until the car vibrated with Reba singing "Fancy." Lily sang along, not caring that her voice was terrible, and that she only hit some of the notes some of the time. She loved singing in the car, and she didn't give a hoot who saw her doing it. She had a long road ahead, and nothing like good old country music to help her along the way.

By the time she reached the tiny town of Jessup, Texas, she was sung out, rung out and starving. The town looked like a hundred others in South Texas. The biggest single store was the grain and feed. Then a Wells Fargo branch. There was an antique store next to a gun shop, and next to that Pete's Dry Cleaning. Then she spied a little diner, Josie's, and she pulled around back to the parking lot. She'd purposely waited to eat until she arrived in Cole Bishop's town. Waitresses in small-town diners could be a wealth of information.

She peeled herself off the seat then shut the door; her car looked a little worse for wear, but that wasn't because of this trip. It had only taken six hours to get here from the ranch. The sports car was almost ten years old, and the Texas weather had beaten down the old broad. But there were some good years left in her. At least, Lily hoped so.

She ran her fingers through her hair, straightened her blouse and skirt and headed inside.

It took her a moment to adjust to the dim light after so much bright sunshine. But once she did, she felt as if she'd been there before. It was a familiar setup, typical of diners all over the country. Four or five booths, a few tables, a counter, a small soda fountain. The waitresses wore jeans and T-shirts with white aprons slung low on their hips. The other truly Texas touch was the preponderance of Stetsons on the clientele.

Lily headed to the middle seat at the counter, between a wiry old cowboy who looked as if he slept in his boots and a middle-aged woman eating a salad, her paperback book open behind her plate.

The waitress, Ginny, according to her name tag came to Lily with a menu and a smile. "Afternoon."

"Hi."

"You headin' to Fort Worth?"

Lily shook her head. "Nope. But maybe you can help me?"

"I'll do what I can."

"First, I need some chicken-fried steak."

"Smart girl. There's none better in the county."

"Excellent. And I'll have an iced tea, please."

Ginny wrote the order, then turned and put it on a clip in the window opening to the kitchen. She poured the tea, gave the cowboy some fresh coffee and came back to Lily. "So what else can I help you with?"

Lily guessed her age at about forty, give or take. Her short cropped hair had some gray in it, her eyes had laugh wrinkles and so did her smile. It was obvious she liked the idea of a stranger in town, with all new stories to tell. Lily sent up a mental thank-you to the patron saint of private detectives, if there was one. "I'm looking for someone. His name is Cole Bishop."

Ginny's pencil slipped from her fingers. The woman to Lily's right snapped her book shut. The cowboy pushed back his Stetson. The reactions were startling, to say the least.

"Are you here for the job?"

Lily had no idea what the job might be, but it seemed a likely avenue to pursue. She couldn't imagine what could cause such a stir. "Yeah. You know anything about it?"

Ginny glanced meaningfully at the woman with the book. The best Lily could figure, the waitress was either scandalized or jealous, or else she had an upset stomach. Finally looking back at Lily, Ginny shook her head. "I don't know that much about it."

Right. "Whatever you can tell me would be great. I'm not sure I got all the details."

The woman shrugged a what-the-hell. "I'll tell you one thing. He's a stunner."

"A stunner?"

"Best-looking man I've ever seen in the flesh."

"I see," she said, although of course, she didn't. What did his looks have to do with the job? Dammit, she shouldn't have said she was going after the job. Now it was impossible to ask straight out what it was.

"And Lord knows he could have any woman he wanted just by crooking his little finger."

The woman next to Lily nodded her agreement. "You'd think he'd want to do things the regular way, wouldn't you?"

Have any woman? The regular way?

"So, tell me something, sweetie," Ginny asked, lowering her voice. "Why on earth would a beautiful young woman like you want to do it?"

It? What was it? "Uh, you know. The usual reasons."

"Usual? I don't know where you're from, child, but in this part of the world, there ain't no usual in what Cole Bishop's up to."

Shit! "Well, that's the thing. I was hoping to learn more about it before I went to see him. *If* I go to see him."

Ginny leaned forward and opened her mouth, but the little bell from the kitchen drew her away before she could say one word. It ended up being Lily's lunch that was ready, and once Ginny retrieved it, she seemed ready to spill the beans. To make sure the waitress knew she had the floor, Lily quickly cut a big slice of the meat and shoved it in her mouth. What she should have done first was make sure it wasn't scorching hot. But she just smiled through the pain as she chewed.

Ginny opened her mouth again, but for the second time, she was interrupted.

"I heard that Stephanie Davidson went by his place about two weeks ago." The woman to Lily's right leaned forward. "She said he was a regular son of a you-know-what."

"I do, Patsy, I do." Ginny shook her head and frowned. "He 'bout bit my head off a couple days back. Just because his coffee wasn't hot enough."

"That's Cole Bishop for you."

"And yet the women fall at his feet. Except for, you know. That's just plum crazy." Ginny realized what she'd said, and shot Lily an embarrassed glance. "No offense meant."

"None taken." Lily smiled, but her imagination was going hog-wild. Was the man a deviant? A pervert? A talk-show host? Maybe Eve wouldn't want him back in her life. Maybe Lily should get in her car and head on home. *What in hell was this job?*

"I don't know." Patsy took a swallow of her iced tea, probably just to add to the drama of the moment. Even after she put down her glass, she hesitated. "I think what the man needs is a good woman. Someone who can turn him around."

"Wait a minute. Are you saying he's gay?"

Ginny shook her head at Lily's question. "Not so's you'd notice. He sees a waitress out at Hastings from time to time. And don't she like to brag about it. According to her, he's got the biggest—"

The kitchen bell rang, and Ginny hustled to the window before she finished the sentence. Lily figured she knew what was so big about Mr. Bishop, but in cattle country one could never be quite sure.

"Manny sure does speak highly of him, though," Patsy said the moment Ginny returned from her waitressing duties.

"Who's Manny?" Lily asked.

"He works for Bishop. Young man, real polite. He's got a girl, Rita Borrego is her name, and she works at the Millers' place. She's a cook and pretty as a petunia."

Lily didn't care about petunias. She wanted to know what was going on with Cole. It was a nightmare version of twenty questions, and Lily's turn was about up. "So, about this job…"

"Jessica Tanksley," Patsy said, as if Lily hadn't spoken. "She's my sister's boyfriend's cousin. She went out there." Patsy looked up to heaven for a moment, then back down. "He looked her over like he was buying a prize heifer. Asked her about a million questions. Real personal, if you get my meaning. But she must have answered wrong. The man never did call her."

This was getting weirder by the second. Not to mention more frustrating. What kind of a job was this? He'd looked the woman over like a cow? Asked personal questions? "What about family?" Lily asked, deciding to approach things from a different angle. "His, I mean."

Ginny's brow rose. "The last person who asked Cole Bishop about his family came down with a sudden case of broken nose and cracked ribs."

"Oh, my."

"My aunt Maureen says he's got a closet full of skeletons." Patsy lowered her voice. "She heard he killed a man."

Lily's mouth dropped open. She hadn't considered that he might be a cold-blooded killer. On the other hand, murder was a damn hard thing to hide. If he'd—

"I'm not saying it's true. But that's what she heard. That he killed a man in cold blood and never gave it another thought."

"Forgive me, Patsy, but your aunt Maureen's crazy as a bedbug."

"She's only been in the hospital that once."

Ginny's hands went to her hips. "It just ain't natural, that's all." She gave Lily a probing look. "And even though it's none of my business, I think you should get in that car of yours and keep on driving. Go on to Fort Worth. Get yourself a real job and find yourself a nice man. Girl like you doesn't need to be messing with the likes of Cole Bishop."

Lily was tempted to do just that. All this talk of unnatural acts had given her the willies. But the willies had never stopped her before. Besides, she knew a thing or two about small-town gossip. Most of what she'd heard this afternoon was probably hogwash. She'd feel a lot better, however, knowing which parts were true. *Just what in hell was this job?*

DYLAN CHECKED OUT a tall blond beauty as she walked down Crockett. He had his sunglasses on, so his perusal was private. As she crossed the street, he jerked his mind back to the business at hand. Sebastian was probably waiting for him downstairs.

He headed toward a huge wooden pushcart with the famous green awning. Perk at the Park, an outdoor coffee bar on the River Walk. Sure enough, there was Sebastian sitting in his usual spot under the brown umbrella. He looked like hell.

Dylan stopped at the pushcart and waited for Kelly Adams, the owner of Perk, to finish her last order. She looked pretty this afternoon, but then she always looked pretty. Maybe it was time for him to do something about his social life. Going out with Kelly would be fun. They'd known each other for a long time, and he felt comfortable with her. She was no Julie but—

He nipped that thought in the bud. Julie's husband sat waiting for him, and the poor guy was nearly out of his mind with worry. Sebastian needed his friendship now. And his total concentration.

"What'll it be, Dylan? The usual?"

He shook his head. "Iced coffee, if you've got some fresh."

"Of course I do. Heavens." She wiped her hands on her apron and turned to fetch his drink.

From the back, Dylan could see her jeans and the small T-shirt she wore. She really was attractive. Maybe, when he'd found Julie, when his life wasn't so crazy...

"Here you go." She handed him the tall plastic cup. "And do me a favor? Cheer up your buddy there, huh? He's got me worried."

"Me, too." He handed her a five. "Thanks, Kelly."

"Hey, your change."

"Keep it," he said over his shoulder.

Sebastian glanced up at him with worried eyes. His hair, usually meticulous, looked as if he hadn't put a comb to it. His smile was a pitiful attempt.

"Hey, ya bastard." Dylan used the old greeting, but it didn't change Sebastian's expression.

"Anything new?"

Dylan shook his head. "Have you slept at all?"

Sebastian shrugged. "I don't sleep through the night anymore. Not like I used to. I end up watching the damn weather channel all night. Go ahead, ask me about tomorrow's high."

"Man, you've got to do something. Have you seen a doctor? Maybe he can give you a sleeping pill."

"Nope. I've thought of it, but it would be too tempting to get dependent on them. I'm not drinking much, either. I need to be clear about things. On my toes."

"Well, I think a couple nights' good sleep would go a long way."

Sebastian looked at the river for a long moment. He sipped his coffee, then put the cup down. "I found a note from Julie last night."

Dylan sat up straight, his heart lurching in his chest. "A note?"

"Don't get too excited. It wasn't a recent note. It was from Christmas. She'd written me a little thank-you for her gift and stuck it in my sock drawer. Except it got caught in the back, and I only saw it today because I yanked the damn drawer out by mistake."

"What did it say?"

He leaned to his right and pulled his leather wallet out of his back pocket. With agonizing slowness, he opened the billfold and brought out a small piece of paper. He put his wallet back, then unfolded the paper. It was all Dylan could do not to rip it out of his hands.

It turned out, he didn't need to. Sebastian handed him the note.

Her handwriting jolted him. He hadn't realized how well he'd known the beautiful script. "Sebastian," the note read. "I love you so. The locket is worth everything to me. I'll never take it off. Never."

Dylan folded the small piece of paper and handed it to his friend. "Son of a bitch."

Sebastian turned to him, his gaze hard and cold. "You have no idea."

"It's not your fault. I know you want it to be, but it's not."

His friend's laugh sent a chill down Dylan's back. There was such self-hatred, such mockery in the hollow tone.

"I should have been with her."

"You were at work."

"It doesn't matter. I should have been with her and I should have protected her. I wanted her to get a gun, but she wouldn't hear of it. She said she'd probably end up shooting herself. I told her we'd go to the range so she could learn how to use a pistol, but then, I don't know, I got busy. I got a new client... I never brought it up again."

"Sebastian, you have to stop this. It's going to drive you insane."

"What's wrong with that?"

"Nothing. Except Julie's coming back. She is. Do

you want to be here when she does? Or in the nut-house?''

"How can you be so certain?''

"Remember when we were in Houston at that rodeo? The one where you got the wild bull—what the hell was his name?''

"Goliath?''

"Yeah. Goliath. And I told you to change your gloves?''

Sebastian nodded. "I didn't listen.''

"And the gloves tore.''

"The rope ripped my hand to shreds.''

"Well, like I knew about the rope, I know about Julie.''

"You are one weird bastard, you know that, Garrett?''

Dylan nodded. "Why else would I hang out with you?''

Sebastian smiled. And for the first time since Julie's disappearance, Dylan felt it was real. But it was gone all too soon, and the cloud of darkness resettled over his best friend.

"I want to go over everything again.'' Dylan got a small notepad from his back pocket. "Step by step.''

"I've told you everything I know.''

"Then tell me again.''

Sebastian sighed. Closed his eyes. And started from the beginning.

CHAPTER FOUR

LILY SLOWED the car as she drove up Cole Bishop's drive. The two-story ranch house reminded her of her cousin Ted's in Waco. The wide front porch had room for a swing or a rocking chair, but it was bare. Painted white, the house itself seemed relatively new, a plain canvas with nothing to distinguish itself.

The lawn was the same. Rye grass, green even in this heat. No flower beds, no hedges. A big oak saved the view from being nondescript.

She wondered if she shouldn't just write him a letter. It wasn't easy to admit, but the conversation from the diner had her a little spooked.

Of course, her dilemma might be solved with a knock on the door. He probably wasn't home. She hoped he wasn't home.

As soon as she opened her car door, she could hear cattle lowing in the distance. It was a familiar sound, one she'd lived around her whole life. Some people would comment on the odor, but she didn't mind it. Folks from cattle country were exposed early to the downside of ranching. It was only the city folk who balked.

She got out, shut the door behind her and opened her purse. After a fresh coat of lipstick, she ran a brush through her hair and popped a mint in her mouth.

As she turned toward the front door, something else familiar, a feeling, not a scent, hit her in the solar plexus. Ever since she'd joined the FBI she'd learned about the combination of fear and excitement that came with a new case. She felt in no personal danger. It wasn't like some of her assignments in the Bureau. But there were high stakes, and she'd have to be alert and aware of everything. Cole Bishop was an unknown, and from the descriptions she'd heard in the diner, he could be anything from Wild Bill Hickok to Hannibal Lecter.

Well, she could be as macho as the next ex-FBI agent. After one last look at her car and safety, she headed toward the porch. No boards squeaked, another sign that they hadn't been here long.

She rang the doorbell and waited, taking calming breaths as she did so. A moment later, the door swung open and Cole Bishop stood before her. It had to be him.

He was on a cell phone, and after giving her a quick once-over, he waved her inside. As she walked past him she was instantly aware of the man's size. And something more. He wasn't just tall, he was powerful. Her gaze went to his biceps, and even beneath his white shirt she could see his arms were thick and corded. Not like a bodybuilder's, though. Like a man at the peak of physical perfection.

He didn't smell half bad, either.

She walked into a sparse living room. Bare white walls, hardwood floor, a leather couch and matching club chairs. The coffee table didn't even have a magazine on it. It was odd, as if Bishop rented the place.

"I don't think that's such a good idea."

His voice startled her and she whirled around, wondering what she'd done wrong. But he wasn't talking to her. Still on the phone, he paced across the floor in his cowboy boots, worn button-fly jeans, his white shirtsleeves rolled up past his elbows. Power. In the way he strode, in his posture, in the way his voice flowed deep and smooth as fine whiskey. She felt a little shiver as he eyed her before turning back to his conversation.

Ginny had said he was the best-looking man she'd ever seen in the flesh, and Lily concurred. Over six feet tall, he had to weigh almost two hundred pounds, all muscle. His tousled brown hair hung over his collar, and when he stepped in front of the window she could see streaks of sun-dyed blond. He had the face of a Marlboro Man, a real cowboy, tough and masculine from the inside out. Even his ocean-blue eyes had a hint of steel in them.

Her gaze moved to his chest and she wondered how he'd look without his shirt on. It took her a moment to realize he'd finished his conversation and put the phone down.

He narrowed his focus to her and only her. Unabashed and brazen as hell, he looked her over from the top of her head to the tips of her toes, taking a little extra time when he got to the chest area. Just as she opened her mouth to protest, he walked behind her.

She tried to swing around, but his hand on her arm stopped her still. Her natural instinct was to jerk away, to defend herself, but she held back. She didn't want to blow this in the first five minutes. But if he didn't let her go in about two seconds, she was going to make sure he understood what gelding was all about.

"How old are you?"

"Pardon me?"

"I said, how old are you?"

That's when it dawned on her that he must have assumed she was here about the position. *The job,* whatever it might be. In that split second she decided to play along, at least for now. At least until she figured out if he was truly dangerous. "I'm thirty."

"Bit old to start having children, isn't it?"

Having children? "No, I don't think so." Her voice sounded normal, she felt sure. Well, almost normal.

"What about illnesses. You have any?"

"None."

"You sure?"

"Of course I'm sure."

"What about your hand?"

She touched her bandage. "A bite. Nothing serious. Just a frightened dog, that's all."

He came around in front of her again, and this time he studied her face. But not in the usual sense. His eyes narrowed as he examined her inch by inch, like a plastic surgeon looking for flaws. Heat warmed her cheeks, but she kept her expression neutral. The thing that frightened her most was that she wanted him to like what he saw.

"How about your teeth?"

This was getting ridiculous. "How about yours?"

"That's not relevant."

"Why not?"

"Because I'm the one with the checkbook."

"But—"

"But nothing. If I decide you're the right one to

have my child, then you can ask me questions. I'll decide then if I want to answer you."

"Your child?" she whispered.

"Make no mistake about it. Even though you'll be the child's mother, that role will be temporary. He's going to be my son, and I alone will make all the decisions affecting his future. The marriage will be for his sake, so he won't be born a bastard, but trust me, you will not be my wife."

Dear Lord...

"So...?" he queried.

"Huh?"

He lowered his head, but not his gaze, and it made him look like a professor addressing a backward student. "Your teeth."

"They're great. My dentist sends me fan letters."

He coughed, but she didn't care. If she'd gotten it right, he wanted to hire a woman to get married, have his child, then leave. My God. He was a loon. Or worse.

"What about—"

She held up a hand. "Hold it."

Impatience drew his brows together.

"You're not the only one who has some decisions to make here, buster."

"Buster?"

She nodded. "Yeah. This will be my kid, after all. And even though you'll have custody, there's nothing you can do to take away my part in this. Besides, anything could happen to you. You could get shot by an irate female, and then where would I be?"

"You—"

"I'd be raising the kid, that's where. Therefore, I'll

need to make sure you're not swimming in the shallow end of the gene pool.''

He didn't say anything, but there was a glimpse of something that might have been a smile. Or a murderous gleam. Whatever it was lasted about one hot second and was replaced by a scowl, which seemed to be his natural mien.

"Do you work out regularly?" he asked, as if she hadn't just finished her tirade.

"I keep fit."

He nodded, his gaze moving to her hips. "Any history of mental illness in your family?"

"Just the usual. An agoraphobic aunt. A cousin who prefers cats to people, which is becoming more understandable every second."

No reaction. At least his gaze moved back to her face. "Did you bring your medical records?"

"Whoa. Not so fast. We're not even close to the medical records portion of this deal. I've got some questions of my own now."

His mouth pressed into a thin line. But he nodded. Once.

She took advantage of the opportunity and gave him a slow perusal, purposefully lingering when she reached his fly. She shook her head a little and creased her brow, as if he hadn't met her standards. She took her time walking around him, touched his upper arm, nodded. Then, to make sure he understood who he was dealing with, she patted his butt.

"Hey." He spun around to face her.

"Just checking."

He took a deep breath, and she could see him struggle to calm down. The crazy thing about this was that he didn't look crazy. Or dangerous. In a bad mood, yes, but that wasn't illegal in Texas. He seemed like a normal, if too good-looking, man. So why in hell did he need to buy a wife and child?

This was getting really interesting.

Bishop shook his head and stepped away. "This interview is over."

Dammit. She couldn't lose him this fast. Eve would be heartsick. No way could Lily live with that kind of guilt. And no way could she leave without getting to the bottom of this very odd situation. "Don't dismiss me just because I've got an attitude. In my experience, it comes in real handy."

"What kind of experience would that be?"

She relaxed, but not much. "I haven't had a lot of luck with men. In fact, I've pretty much had it with the whole gender. What I'm looking for is something with no complications. I want to write, and I want to be left alone. But I need to eat, too."

"Write what?"

"Novels."

He nodded. "How did you hear about me?"

Okay, she'd gotten her reprieve. Now she had to hang on to it. "Ginny at the diner told my aunt and she told me."

Bishop checked his watch, then looked out the window. At what, Lily couldn't see.

"Come sit down." There was no politeness in his statement, no niceties about the man at all as far as she could tell. He led her to a large kitchen, which was just as blah as the living room. Of course he didn't hold her chair for her. The only thing he did that was the least bit courteous was nod at the fridge. "There are drinks in there."

"Thank you for your gracious offer, but I'm fine."

She winced at her stupid big mouth. This was no time to antagonize the man.

He ignored the jab. He just grabbed a thick file from the sideboard. It had no markings on the outside, but she gathered it was his Child Bearer folder.

"This is the deal." He didn't open the file. He just looked her right in the eyes as he laid it out. "I don't want a wife. I want a child. My child. The only reason a woman has to be involved at all is to bear the child and care for him until he's old enough for me to tend him. I've decided to marry the woman I choose, but there will be no married life. I want my son to have every opportunity. And no strikes against him out of the gate."

"And if it's a daughter?"

"That's okay, too. None of this is negotiable. Trust me, the financial arrangement will allow you to do all the writing you want. The only thing is, when the child is old enough, you leave."

"What about visitation?"

He turned away for a moment, and she saw his jaw flex. "I haven't decided about that yet."

"Is it my turn?"

"Go ahead."

"First, how do you plan on me conceiving this child?"

"I have a doctor lined up for in-vitro fertilization."

"You'll pay for everything? Insurance? Clothes?" He nodded.

"What about spending money?"

"You don't have to worry about that. I'll make sure you want for nothing."

"No offense, but how do I know you have enough

money to back up that offer? Your spread is no King Ranch."

"If it gets to that point, I'll give you access to my financial statements."

She eyed him long and hard, still amazed at the proposition. Now she understood why Ginny and Patsy had been so alarmed. It would have been better if she hadn't needed to lie, but given the circumstances, she forgave herself. This was the most bizarre arrangement she'd ever heard of. Naturally, she wanted to bring Cole home to Eve, but, her own curiosity was now so great it would take a crowbar to pry her out of here. "I'll stay for a week."

"Excuse me?"

"I said, I'll stay. But only on a trial basis. I'm not walking in here without knowing you better, and that's final. This is a major decision for me."

"How do you know I'm even considering you for the job?"

She smiled. "How many other women have gotten to this stage of the interview process?"

"Several."

"And how many told you that you were out of your ever-loving mind?"

He flipped open his file and the jaw twitched again. "We'll try it for three days. If you check out."

"If I check out how?"

"I'm going to investigate you, Ms...." His brows creased and his nostrils flared. "What the hell is your name?"

"I thought you'd never ask. It's Lily. Lily Garrett."

He handed her a job application form. "Fill out the personal information."

"Fine. But I need to make a phone call. If I'm staying, I have to let certain people know."

He handed her his cell phone.

She flipped it open and dialed all but one number, then gave him a pointed look. "Do you mind?"

"No."

"Fine." She got up and headed for the living room. At least Bishop didn't follow her. Dylan answered on the second ring.

"Listen," she said, making sure Bishop couldn't hear her. "I'll explain later, but someone's going to be doing a check on me. Make me sound like I'm your flaky sister, and your secretary. Bad secretary. Tell them I want to be a writer. Say I earn about fifteen grand a year, and if it gets real chatty, say I've had a couple of lousy relationships."

"What in hell—"

"I'll call you. Bye." She clicked off the connection and turned to find Cole on his feet, halfway to her. "All done," she said, holding out the phone for him.

"Who was that?"

"Not that it's any of your business, but it was my brother. I told him I'd be gone a week."

He took his phone back. "I'll show you to your room."

She smiled at him. Her most dazzling grin. But he just turned around and walked toward the hall.

COLE KNEW he was making a grievous error even as he led the woman toward the back of the house. First, she had a mouth on her, and he sure as hell didn't need that. But her attitude wasn't half as disturbing as the effect she had on his libido.

She was too attractive. While that should be a plus

in her favor, it presented some significant issues. If he chose her, she'd live here for several years. They were sure to run into each other, even though he'd make absolutely certain they didn't get personally involved on any level.

If he could have raised an infant by himself, this wouldn't even be an issue. He'd thought about hiring a nanny, but he'd read too much about the initial mother-child bond to want to risk that with his child. Besides, he needed to have someone with a vested interest in sticking around. His last five housekeepers had quit in rapid succession, and so had the last three cooks. It was so damn hard to get good help these days.

He heard her behind him as he opened the door to the guest room. Unfortunately, he made the mistake of being a "gentleman" and let her pass while he held the door. Her scent hit him hard. Flowers. Flowers and female, that's what she smelled like. The female part was far more interesting than the flowers.

"This will do."

She stood in the middle of the room, her arms folded as she checked out her living quarters. He took the opportunity to look at her—this time, not as a potential mother, but as a woman.

Her height was good. He guessed she was five eight or nine. A real Thoroughbred, too, her long slender legs shown off well by her fitted skirt. Her blouse wasn't form fitting, and yet he could see the shape and size of her breasts. He liked what he saw. Not too large. Just right.

He had to admit he liked the hair, too. Long, almost to her waist, and black as the midnight sky. But the worst of his problems was her face.

She had the kind of beauty that could make a man do foolish things. Her clear green eyes were intelligent and observant. Her lips, full and lush, seemed poised to break into a smile. He could guess what her skin felt like. Pure silk. Stunning looks and that smart-ass attitude of hers—he could see why she'd had trouble with men. Most men would want to possess a woman like her. Most men wouldn't stand a chance.

"Who's your decorator?" she asked. Now she was by the armoire, opening the drawers one by one.

"No decorator. I furnished the place."

She gave him a mocking glance. "Really?"

"I haven't had the time for anything but the necessities."

"Right. Because of your vast financial empire. I forgot."

"Look, if you don't—"

"Wait." She held up her hands. "I didn't mean that. It was very rude of me. I guess I'm just tired, that's all. I've been on the road all day."

"From?"

"Just outside San Antonio."

"You work there?"

She nodded. "For my brother's small private investigation firm. Finders Keepers. I take care of the office. You know, filing, computer work, that sort of thing."

"You don't like it?"

"I do. But it's a full-time job that doesn't pay a hell of a lot."

The alarm on his wristwatch went off, and he silenced it with a quick flick of his finger. He didn't want to leave. He wanted to find out more about Lily Garrett. A great deal more.

But there wasn't time now. "You brought your things with you?"

"They're in the car."

He nodded, turned and headed back down the hall, leaving the scent of the woman behind him. He'd let her stay, at least for tonight, but she wasn't going to work out. Which was too damn bad, because he didn't have another prospect in sight.

The plan was sound. He'd get everything he wanted. A child. A woman he'd control with his checkbook. No complications. What he hadn't counted on was how difficult his search for the right woman would be. Most of the applicants had been completely unacceptable. Those who came close either hadn't passed the background check or clearly wanted the marriage to be a traditional one.

At least Lily hadn't balked at his proposition. Maybe it would have been better if she had.

He passed through the kitchen and went out the back door. The heat hit him like a slap in the face, but he just kept walking. One of the bulls had hurt his leg yesterday, and the vet was due. After that, he needed to talk to Manny and find out how the new feed was working out.

Halfway to the paddock, he found himself thinking about the woman. The curve of her breasts, the way her legs went on and on. An ache came over him. It had been too long since he'd had a woman. Which was another reason he shouldn't have let her stay.

If there was one thing on earth he wished for more than a son, it was to stop feeling this need. Most times, he could push the desire out of his head, and when he couldn't, there were some willing waitresses in Jessup and Hastings to ease the pain.

But he hated that part of himself. It made him weak. Vulnerable. He never wanted to be vulnerable around a woman again. When he was hard, his head got soft. He got stupid.

Not this time. If he didn't stop thinking about her, he'd tell her to leave tonight.

CHAPTER FIVE

LILY CLOSED the bedroom door, took a peek out the window to make sure no one was lurking outside, and called Dylan on her cell phone. He picked up before the phone rang.

"Lily?"

"Yeah." She didn't bother to ask him how he'd known. This little magic trick had happened before.

"What the hell was that last call about?"

"Okay." She sank down on the bed, happily discovering it was firm, but not too. "You're never going to believe this." She went on to tell him about Cole Bishop's proposition, pausing only to let Dylan ask a question here and there. By the time the whole story was out, she was back on her feet, at the bedroom's other door. She rapped softly, and when no one answered, she opened it slowly, somehow expecting to see Rochester's wife or a reasonable facsimile.

"Lily?"

"Hang on." She peeked behind the door then sighed with relief. "How interesting."

"Excuse me? Do I need to be on the phone for this?"

"Yes. I just found the nursery."

"Boy, he's a positive thinker, isn't he?"

"I'll say. And here's the really fascinating part."

She walked over to the gorgeous antique crib. "The room is completely decorated. Murals on the wall, pictures, cute little puppy lamps and sheets and curtains."

"Why is that so fascinating?"

"No other room in the house is done. Not like this. I mean it. There isn't one picture on a wall, not one tchotchke at all. Zippo."

"Maybe the decorator hasn't finished yet."

"He doesn't have one. He told me."

"So, it's clear this guy is willing to go to some pretty serious lengths to have a child. What worries me is why."

She shook her head as she ran a hand over a huge stuffed tiger propped in the corner. "That worries me, too. So how about you do a little digging on him while he's doing a little digging on me?"

Dylan sighed. "Sure, why not."

"Uh-oh. Things not going well with Julie's case?"

"You could say that. I swear, Lily, the woman just vanished off the face of the earth. I know it doesn't seem possible, but I'm hitting my head against brick wall after brick wall."

"Nothing in the police reports?"

"Not that I've seen. And remember Eddy Baskin?"

"The cop from Dallas?"

"He's down here now, and he gave me the real scoop. Truth is, the PD isn't doing any better."

"I have faith in you, Dylan. If anyone can find her—"

"That's the problem. Can she be found? I don't know."

"It's too soon for that kind of attitude, little brother."

"I'm okay. It's Sebastian I'm concerned about. He looks like hell."

"Well, then that makes it even more important for you to think positively. You have to believe you're going to find her, Dylan. She needs you, and so does Sebastian."

"Right."

"You know what?"

"What?"

"There are baby clothes in the drawers."

"Who *is* this guy?"

"Got me. But we're going to find out, aren't we?"

"You be careful, huh? If he's a creep—"

"I've met creeps before, Dylan. And I know how to handle myself."

"Of course you do. But it's a brother's prerogative to worry. Oh, I told Dad you'd be gone for a few days."

"Thanks. Hey, have you called about an assistant yet?"

"Nope. But I will if you stop talking."

"Bye." She hung up and continued her investigation of the nursery. It truly was a lovely room. The walls, the palest blue, were bordered in the puppy motif, which was completely adorable. The carpet the same eggshell color as in the rest of the house, but in here, the pile was twice as thick.

He'd gone to a lot of trouble to make this room perfect. She'd never seen a man want a child like this. Not a man alone, at least.

Her friend Irene and her husband Don had been trying to have a child for three years. Last time they'd talked, Don had broken down completely. He felt utterly desperate and was talking about going to a sperm bank, but it was clear the idea humiliated him. He wanted a baby like this. Like Cole.

She could only hope that Cole's intentions were honorable. But the truth was, she'd seen too much in her FBI days to think all people were motivated by high standards and morals. Especially devilishly handsome men.

Dylan would find out if there was anything hinky about Cole. Any criminal record or a hint of impropriety. Even though it was prudent to think this unorthodox arrangement wasn't kosher, Lily had a feeling about Cole. He was odd, that was for certain, but she knew somehow he wasn't doing anything illegal.

After she'd retrieved her suitcase from the car, she went back into her room. She'd brought clothes for a week, but she couldn't imagine being here that long. Heck, she might be gone by tonight. Especially if she kept goading him the way she had. The smart thing to do would be to shut up and agree with the man, whatever he said. But she could have sworn she'd seen something in his eyes when they were sparring. A hint of interest, of curiosity. Her intuition was telling her that Cole needed a challenge. She'd give him one. Unfortunately, there was a fine line between a challenge and a pain in the ass. She'd just have to feel her way because she needed to find out a few things about Mr. Bishop. Eve was counting on her.

He'd thank her in the end. She knew that, too. It was getting to the end that was tricky.

She took out her journal and put it in the drawer of the bedside table along with her favorite purple pen. Next to them went her antibiotics, her birth control pills—which she could not believe she was still taking, except that they were good for her complexion—and a big juicy novel. Since there was no television in the room, she was happy she'd brought something to read. Of course, she could go exploring. Find out where the television was.

She slammed the drawer shut and headed off to see what she could see.

THE BULL was going to make it. He'd hobble for a week or two in his splint, but there was no serious damage. Not that animals with broken legs were killed anymore. But caring for the monster wouldn't be easy. He was a mean SOB, and Cole and the vet had used some mighty powerful tranquilizers on him before they got close. He was one of the prime studs on the ranch, an award winner with an impeccable lineage.

Cole needed to meet Manny. Then he had correspondence to catch up on and a few phone calls to make. Work enough to last until dinner. But the woman was on his mind.

He stared up at the house as Doc Scott's van spewed dust on its way out. He'd been out here nearly an hour. Too long. He didn't know her. She could be anything. A thief. A con artist. It was foolish to leave her alone.

Manny would have to wait. Besides, he had to fax her information to the private detective he'd hired to do background checks. Just to be on the safe side, though, he'd stay in the house for the rest of the night. His work could wait.

As he neared the back porch, he wondered what

he'd find her doing. Resting? Reading? Maybe taking a shower?

Bad thought. Because with the thought came images. Moving pictures in living color. The steam, her naked body, his mouth on her—

He stopped, took his Stetson off his head and wiped his brow. It was too damn hot. Summer in Jessup was five degrees from hell. The sun beat down from a pale-blue sky with not a tree or a cloud to soften the blow. But Cole didn't mind working up a sweat. Not doing honest work. What he wouldn't do was get himself crazy over a woman—even a woman like Lily Garrett. No matter that her hair glistened or her eyes sparked with intelligence. He wasn't about to let his guard down.

He knew too well how cunning women could be. How sly and manipulative. Oh, he wasn't foolish enough to think all women were like that. He knew there were just as many honest, straightforward women as men. The problem was, he couldn't tell the difference.

He could read a man. Tell a lot about him from his handshake. From his eyes. From the tone of his voice. But he was helpless around the female of the species. Not a feeling he liked.

This woman, this Lily Garrett, was even more dangerous. Half his mind was occupied thinking about that hair of hers. Those legs. She could be selling him the Brooklyn Bridge and he wouldn't know it.

So what in hell was he doing, letting her stay? Was he that desperate, or just stupid?

Dammit, he hadn't thought his life would turn out like this. He'd had it good. The world on a silver platter. But then...

All he wanted was his own little family. Him and his baby. The two of them would build an empire, standing side by side. He'd be what a father should be. Cole Junior would never have to worry about his old man doing him dirt. But first, Cole Senior had to find a woman.

He'd thought about this long and hard, and while it might not be a solution for another man, it suited him. He would be in complete control. His son would look to Cole to see how to grow up. To see what was right and wrong.

Cole headed on again, and this time he wasn't going to be distracted. He needed to find out everything he could about the woman inside, and he needed to do it fast. The rest of his life, and his son's life, depended on him doing this right.

LILY TURNED the page of her journal and continued writing in that frenzied way of hers. When she got like this, when her mind spun twice as fast as her hand could write, her heart pounded and her breathing grew shallow, as if she would die if she didn't get it all on paper. As if her thoughts would disappear unless they were in purple ink.

It was her seventeenth volume. Everything from schoolwork to being a twin, to first love and betrayal was in her journals. She thought of them as her essence, and more than that, her teacher. Putting it all down in writing had helped her in more ways than she could ever say.

Now, sitting cross-legged on this strange bed, her feet curled under her, her hair tied back and her journal on page six, she felt safe. She felt in control. She would bring Cole back to Eve. They would reconcile. She knew it.

"He's got something to hide," she wrote. "Something that ripped him away from his old family and twisted his vision of a new family. It's all tied together. He doesn't want a child so much as he wants someone—family—to love."

Of course, Lily would never share these impressions with anyone else. But it was important not to dismiss them out of hand.

She paused, stretched her neck, gnawed on the end of her pen. Then she shifted her focus back to the present. But instead of thinking about Cole Bishop's dark secret, her thoughts strayed to the breadth of his shoulders. The streaks of blonde in his hair. That cruel mouth... What would it be like to kiss a man like him? So hard. So demanding.

A shiver took her by surprise, and an ache she'd banished came back and settled in down below.

"Oh, no," she said aloud. "No way. I'm not interested in Cole Bishop. Or any man. Not yet."

She turned back to her journal and scribbled furiously, listing all the reasons she had no business thinking about shoulders or kisses. There were a dozen reasons, maybe more. But only one that mattered. She wasn't healed yet. Not by a long shot. To make another mistake might be fatal. Well, maybe not *fatal* fatal. But there were several women she knew well who had been so damaged they'd thrown in the towel. Given up on men completely. She didn't want that for herself.

Someday, she planned to marry. Before she was forty, preferably. This year would be about finding out what she wanted. Who she was. Learning why things had gone so badly in Dallas.

She paused, thinking about how her criteria had changed as she'd gotten older. When she was in her early twenties, the number one thing she wanted was someone gorgeous. The inside of the package hadn't mattered at all. She wanted someone cool and sexy and a little bit dangerous. Then she'd gone through her "deep" phase, where her entire focus was on intellectuals. What a disaster that had been.

In her late twenties, she'd gone for humor. That had been fun, but ultimately unsatisfying. The man she'd been with had been a riot, but his humor was a shield she'd never gotten past.

Then there'd been her married-FBI-agent phase. No, that wasn't fair. She hadn't known. He'd been so right in so many other ways. Funny, intelligent, sexy as hell. The missing ingredients were honesty, obviously, and kindness.

Kindness hadn't been on her list until lately, but now it was right up there at the top. She wanted a man with a good heart. Someone who thought of her first. Just like she'd think of him first.

Who knew? Miracles happened. She might find him. Someday. Certainly not here or now. Good grief. Cole Bishop might be a lot of things, but kind? Highly doubtful.

She heard something. A door shut.

He was back.

She closed her journal and uncurled her legs, disturbingly aware that her pulse had quickened. It probably wasn't anything. Just nerves about the case. She had a lot to find out in a short period of time. And she had to find the right moment to tell Cole the truth about why she was here.

After two deep, slow breaths, she got up, put her journal underneath her underwear in the top drawer of the armoire, then headed out to see Cole.

He was in the kitchen, drinking a tall glass of water. With his head back, his neck caught her attention, and as he swallowed, his Adam's apple rose and fell in such a dramatically masculine way it was only natural that a little shiver would race up her spine. It didn't mean anything.

When he brought the glass down, he wiped his mouth with the back of his arm. Oh, mama, but he was a fine-looking specimen. Purely from an aesthetic perspective, of course.

He stared at her blatantly, not saying a word. His gaze moved over her again, a patient inspection of a different sort from the one a few hours ago. There was heat in his gaze. Almost a hunger, as if he wanted to drink her like that glass of water.

She blinked first. The tension inside her was too strong. "Did you finish your business?"

"Not all of it."

"Are you leaving again?"

He shook his head.

"Why not?"

"I don't want to leave you alone here."

"It's all right. I can amuse myself."

"I don't care about that."

"You don't?"

Again, he gave that slow shake of his head, his gaze never moving an inch.

"What do you care about?"

He swallowed. Looked down her body again, then back to her eyes. "You're a stranger."

"True."

"You might have an agenda I don't know about."

She felt her face heat, and she headed for the refrigerator before he could see her. "What do you mean?" Purposely standing with her back to him, she opened the fridge and searched for a cold drink.

"For all I know, you're a world-class con artist. Maybe you mean to steal me blind."

"I'll forgive the conjecture, but only because you said 'world-class.'"

He moved closer to her. She could feel him behind her, so close it made the hairs on the back of her neck stand up. What did he know? Had her cover already been blown?

"Did anyone ever tell you that flippant attitude of yours could get you in trouble?"

That whiskey voice of his slipped inside her, making her hand tremble as she pulled out a can of soda. He was too close to her. And she was too aware of him. "Everyone's told me that. From my parents to my bosses to my next-door neighbor."

"And you keep it up?"

It was hell trying to focus on this silly conversation while her hormones were going bonkers. What was this? Some kind of a joke? It was as if she'd never been near a man before. She wished she could climb in the vegetable crisper and close the door behind her. But she had to face him. This was business. A tricky business at that. When she did turn, she was immediately sorry to have given up the crisper idea so quickly.

He towered over her, even though he wasn't that

much taller. It was the whole package of the man that made him seem so large. So strong. As if he could snap her like a twig. But that same power suggested something else, something she was a fool to think about. What would it be like to have sex with him? To have him inside her?

She popped open the soda and the noise made her jump. He didn't even blink. He just kept staring at her, his eyes raw with flat-out want.

She lifted the can to her parched lips and took a sip. He watched her mouth, his own lips parting. She'd never seen such a mouth on a man before. His lips were just full enough to make the idea of kissing him alluring, but they were also slender and hard; made for sliding over a woman's curves.

"What do you want, Lily Garrett? Why are you here?"

"I'm applying for the job."

"You think you could handle it? Handle me?"

"That all depends on whether you're a gentleman or not."

He took another step, until his chest brushed her arm. "I'm not."

The cold air behind her and the heat in front met inside her, brewing up one hell of a storm. It wasn't enough he had that rugged cowboy thing going on, but he also oozed bad-boy sexy, which wasn't the least bit fair.

His hand lifted and he touched her hair. Just her hair. And she nearly dropped her soda.

"You're old enough to know better," he whispered.

"Better than what?"

"That you shouldn't play with fire if you don't want to get burned."

She needed to make her mouth work. For words to form. But that seemed way too difficult as his fingers brushed her cheek. "I don't think this is such a good idea."

"What?"

"You touching me."

"I'll stop if you want me to."

She closed her eyes. His thumb, callused and thick, followed the curve of her jaw all the way to her chin. "Stop." Her voice sounded weak, soft.

"Stop this?" he asked. "Or this?" He leaned forward that small bit and kissed her.

It wasn't the hard edge she expected. His lips barely touched hers. His breath slipped inside her as he moved his head back and forth, rubbing her in that one spot. It was maddening and electrifying.

Finally, she couldn't stand it. She leaned in. But at that very second, he stepped back, and when she opened her eyes, his face wore that damned granite mask. As if he hadn't touched her. Hadn't made her crazy inside.

"This isn't going to work," he said, his voice tinged with anger.

She looked down, breaking the connection between them. It had been a test. A stupid— "I don't appreciate being played for a fool, Mr. Bishop."

"I don't think you're a fool."

"No? Then what was all that about? Were you trying to get me to kiss you? To slap you?"

"I wasn't trying anything. If you stay, we're going to be in close quarters. You understand? In the same house, in the same room."

"So what? Do you find me so irresistibly attractive that you're afraid I'll drive you wild? That you won't be able to control yourself when I'm near?"

Finally, his mask cracked. A half smile changed his face, but not for long. He pulled himself together. Almost. He had to take a few steps back to make the shift complete. "I do find you attractive. And that's a problem."

"Well, there's only one answer to that, Cole Bishop."

"What?"

"Get the hell over it."

CHAPTER SIX

COLE BLINKED. It wasn't the response he'd expected. She wasn't what he expected. By now, she should have been packed and halfway to the door. Instead, she stood toe to toe with him, her eyes challenging him to do his worst.

What she didn't understand was what his worst was. And he couldn't tell her. Because his brilliant little plan had backfired. Instead of scaring her away, he'd just put the fear of God in himself.

He'd wanted to kiss her. Hell, he still wanted to kiss her. He wanted to bring her into his arms, and he wanted to touch every inch of that long, lean body. He wanted those legs wrapped around his waist.

She stepped neatly around him, leaving the refrigerator door open. "What time is dinner?"

He should just tell her to go. What was the point in her staying? She'd never work out.

"Dinner?" she prompted. "You know, the meal after lunch?"

"Six-thirty."

"Thanks. See you then."

He closed the fridge, and by the time he'd turned around, she was gone. He leaned back, wondering how things had gotten so out of hand so quickly.

He knew his size intimidated people, and he'd

learned to use it effectively. Sure, Lily was tall, but when he stood close, she must have felt vulnerable.

He also knew his stare unnerved even the most secure individuals if he wanted it to. And he had. But Lily had kept her cool. At least, for the most part. There had been a few moments there...

Shit. He needed his head examined. In the meantime, he had a couple of things to do. Fax her application to the detective, and then take a long, cool shower.

LILY CLOSED her bedroom door, then slumped against it, her heart beating frenziedly against her chest. "I am in *so* much trouble here. And I've only known him three hours."

She pushed off the door and flung herself across the bed. That little tango in the kitchen had nearly done her in. The jerk had some nerve testing her like that. For all he knew, she was going to be the mother of his child. It wasn't nice and it wasn't fair, and oh, my God, how she'd flunked.

This attraction to him was something outside of her experience. It made her feel foolish about Jason, which was perhaps the most damning evidence. In all the time she'd been with Jason, including that heady rush at the beginning, her body had never reacted like it just had with Cole.

She turned over and looked down at her boobs. "Bad body," she scolded. But there were no immediate apologies. Maybe she should call Dylan and talk it over with him. No. This was not something she wished to discuss with her brother. Ashley? Uh-uh. Somehow, somewhere, it would come back and bite her on the butt.

The other options were her two closest girlfriends, Denise and Sandy, but Denise was in Europe on a business trip and Sandy was too much in love with Paul, her babe du jour, to give sensible advice.

What a pickle. The intelligent thing would be to march out there, tell Cole that she was a private detective, that she'd been sent by Eve, yada, yada, yada. Then he'd tell her exactly what she could do with Finders Keepers, and she'd be staying at the Jessup Motel.

Plan B? Keep her wits about her, find out all she could about Cole, and when the time was right, explain the situation if it seemed prudent. If he really was a nutball, she didn't want to turn him on Eve.

And then there was Plan C. Which was forget about the case, forget about her vow to stay chaste until she was completely over Jason, and attack Cole in the middle of the night. Make love until the paramedics were called, then spring her true mission on him when he was too weak to argue.

Plan C had some merit. She just wished she'd paid attention when Sandy had talked about rebound guys. There was something every woman should know about meeting men right after a big breakup, but for the life of her, Lily couldn't remember what it was. Sleep with them? Don't sleep with them? It was one of the two.

My goodness, but this was not how she thought her day was going to go. However, there was a little part of her that was unapologetically excited. Curious as hell about what was going to happen next. She honestly didn't know. Would he make another move? Would he ignore her?

She had the feeling if he really meant to kick her

out she would have been kicked by now. No, despite the Granite Man demeanor, the guy was probably as confused as she was.

Wanting to hire a wife. For heaven's sake. What a dumb thing to do. Maybe she was supposed to be here to knock some sense into the big guy. Show him that he couldn't be in control of everything. And that money and the love of a mother didn't mix.

Sighing, she sat up, looked at the clock. Another forty minutes and it would be dinner. She was definitely hungry. But there was time to shower, to cool herself down and gather her composure. Assuming, that is, that she could stop thinking about those shoulders.

FROM THE VOICES, she guessed there were about five people in the dining room. Five men, to be more precise. One of them, presumably, was Cole Bishop.

Maybe she should go back and change into her dress. And her Manolo strappy sandals. She'd learned in the last few years that she had a powerful weapon in her body. Not that she was Rachel Ravishing or anything, but when she played it right, her body could be downright distracting. It wasn't surprising, really. Men had very little willpower when it came to the promise, no matter how remote, of sex. So why shouldn't she use that fact to her advantage?

She turned back, then stopped. It wasn't necessary to play the game on that level. Sure, he'd gotten to her with that almost-kiss, but that didn't mean she had to pay him back in kind. She had a job to do, and nothing in her mission required showing a little thigh.

Besides, it wasn't clothes that made the woman,

right? It was attitude. Confidence. Since she'd decided to stick with Plan B, she needed to forget about everything but doing the job. Getting what she wanted quickly and efficiently. He could only intimidate her if she let him. She straightened her shoulders, undid one more button on her blouse, and walked into the dining room like she was Cindy friggin' Crawford.

It was a stunner of an entrance. She hadn't needed the dress at all. With her hair down, her makeup just right, the hint of décolleté, she owned the damn room. All conversation ceased. A man in a stained white hat let go of his spoon. Several jaws dropped. Someone swore just under his breath. The only problem was, Cole wasn't there to see it.

She pasted on a smile as she walked up to the closest cowboy and extended her hand. "I'm Lily Garrett."

The man was older, perhaps in his early sixties, with a thick head of white hair. He wore glasses and he looked at her through the lower part of his lenses. "Pleased to meet ya," he said, his Texas accent as thick as spring mud. The hand she shook felt rough and warm. His jeans and shirt were both dusty, as were his boots. But the huge rectangular belt buckle around his waist was so shiny she needed sunglasses.

"I'm Chigger," he said. "I'm the stockman here." He nodded to the cowboy on his right. "This here is John. He works with the bull breeding."

"Nice to meet you."

John touched the tip of his hat with his fingers and gave her a friendly nod.

"Manny, come on over here. Meet Lily Garrett. You too, Spence."

Both men obeyed. They were years younger than

Chigger. Manny, an absolutely adorable Latino, looked to be in his early twenties, and Spence, a solemn gent in the only baseball cap in the room, was around her age.

They both said "Hey," and then the whole group of them got real quiet. They didn't stop looking at her, though, and she said a silent thanks that she hadn't put on the dress.

Spence cleared his throat. "Excuse me, miss, but are you the new cook?"

"Me? Oh, no."

The men sighed. Heavily. The hunger in their eyes dulled, and she realized they hadn't been thinking she was a hot mama at all. So much for the powerful weapon of her body. "You don't have a cook?"

"Not since Ellie quit." Chigger hitched up his pants. "She made the best roast chicken I ever ate."

The others nodded. Manny, whose name she remembered from the diner, frowned. "Anything's better than J.T.'s cooking."

"I heard that," a man said from the kitchen. "And you, Manny Peres, are not having any dessert tonight."

"I don't like your lumpy pudding anyway."

"We're not having pudding." The kitchen guy stuck his head out. "We're having ice cream. Everybody but you."

Manny rolled his eyes. "He's full of—"

Chigger coughed, but she still heard the curse word. Not that she hadn't heard it before. She was a rancher's daughter after all. But it was sort of gallant that the old gentleman wanted to protect her delicate ears.

"Now, Lily Garrett." Chigger shoved Manny toward the dining room table. It was sort of set. The silverware was in a jumble in the middle of the table, napkins in a big pile next to that, and plates stacked on the other side. "Just who might you be?" He leaned in close and lowered his voice. "You're not applying for the, uh, other job, are you?"

"Mind your own business, old man."

She whirled around to find Cole standing behind her. His scowl didn't bother her this time. But his nearness did. Her tummy did that strange tightening thing again, and her fingers went to the hollow of her neck.

"You respect your elders," Chigger said, but he didn't press Lily for more information.

Cole had changed clothes. Showered. His hair was still damp, and if she wasn't mistaken, his face freshly shaved. Interesting. Or did he always shower before dinner?

He'd donned another pair of jeans and his slim hips made her think evil thoughts. When her gaze moved up to his chest, things went from bad to worse. She forced herself to turn and look at the other men.

They stood silent and still, gazes moving from Cole to her and back again. It was as if they were on hold, waiting to see what they should do, how they should react.

She understood. It seemed natural to take Cole's emotional temperature and prudent to act accordingly. He wasn't someone you'd want to cross. The only one who was relaxed was Chigger.

"Well, are we gonna stand here all night gawkin' at each other?" the old man asked. "Or are we gonna eat?"

That pushed everyone into motion again. Everyone but her. Cole headed toward her, moving his gaze slowly down her body, then up again. He didn't react, except for rhythmically fisting and loosening his right hand.

She turned her back on him and smiled at the men. "I don't know about anyone else, but I'm famished. Is there something I can do to help with dinner?"

"Cook it," Manny mumbled.

Chigger put his hand on her arm and led her to the table. With a courtly bow, he held the chair for her. "You're our guest, and just because some of us were raised by wolves, that doesn't mean all of us were. What can I get you to drink, young lady?"

"Thank you, sir. I'd love a glass of ice water, if that wouldn't be too much trouble."

"Not at all."

She heard Cole snort from halfway across the room. But she didn't care. It was nice to be treated like a lady. It didn't mean she couldn't put any one of them in a headlock if she had to, but common courtesy was always welcome.

Manny sat down on her right, and Spence hurried to take the seat on her left. She reached for a napkin and some silverware, and then the others followed suit. A few moments later, J.T. came out of the kitchen holding a steaming pot. Stew, with thick chunks of meat and potatoes. A little heavy for this time of year, but it smelled okay.

Chigger showed up behind her and set down her water. Bread—two loaves, store bought—completed the menu. Everyone had taken a seat except Cole.

Another power trip. She recognized it from her

days at the academy. He waited until the silence returned and then, when every eye was upon him, sat at the head of the table.

"I'm reminded of a story," she said, and the focus of the room switched to her. "In France, during the time of Napoleon, it was an incredible breech of etiquette to sit down before the emperor. In fact, being that he was a megalomaniac and a dictator, there were actual protocols written, explaining that the bottoms of the visitors should not touch a chair until the bottom of the emperor touched his. Only Napoleon was a restless sort. So people at his dinner parties kept jumping up and down all night, deathly afraid to have their bottoms in contact with anything inappropriate lest the wrath of the emperor should come down upon them."

No one laughed. They all just looked at Cole again. It was like a tennis match with the score forty-love.

"Pass the lady the stew," Cole said finally.

That broke the ice. The pot was passed as they all grudgingly filled their plates.

"I had a stew once," Manny said wistfully, "made with lamb and fresh-picked carrots and potatoes. Man, that was some stew."

Spence nodded as he looked at the lumpy concoction on his plate. "Remember that roast what's-her-name—the one with the glasses—made?"

The men, except Cole of course, nodded.

"She was a good one," Chigger said. "Mary. That's right. She made those pies, too." He gave Cole a disapproving scowl. "She would have stayed, too. She liked it here."

"She liked the liquor cabinet," Cole said.

Lily decided it was time to try the food. It couldn't be that bad. Stew wasn't that difficult. But the moment she had it in her mouth, she understood all. It was terrible. Not just bland, but actively awful. She just smiled and chewed, not wanting to hurt J.T.'s feelings.

The men beside her had no such qualms. J.T. took their abuse manfully. In fact, he seemed just as displeased with the meal as the others.

Only Cole ate silently. She'd managed to avoid his glare through most of the meal. Finally, she couldn't stand it any longer. She let her gaze slide over to him as he ate. He didn't acknowledge her at all, didn't even realize she was looking his way. At least, so she thought. But a moment later, his hand moved to his chest, and, in a gesture familiar to all history buffs, he slipped it inside the front of his shirt.

She burst out laughing. Once more, the conversation halted. But when the men looked at Cole, his hand was on the table, his expression slightly puzzled, as if he didn't understand her outburst, either. The sly dog.

"YOU STAYING the night?"

As Lily turned to Spence with a smile, Cole swallowed the last of his bread. He hadn't been the least bit hungry, but he'd eaten every bite of the horrible meal. At least the ice cream was good. The dinner had shown him, as if he still needed reasons, just how unsuitable she was for the job. She talked too much, for one thing. And she distracted the men, for another.

What he needed was an old-fashioned ranching

wife. The kind who knew how to work hard, have kids and keep her opinions to herself.

That jab about Napoleon still rankled. Cole might be a lot of things, but a megalomaniac wasn't one of them. He was something of a dictator, but only because that's what running a ranch required. He was proud of his spread and of the way his men respected him. He never asked them to do anything he wouldn't do himself.

But she'd walked in and tipped the scales, and that wasn't going to work at all. Not even for a night.

"Yes," she said, her smile making Spence blush. "I'm staying for a few days. Cole and I are trying to see if we want to work together."

"Doing what?"

"Oh, he wants to pay me to have his baby."

Spence spit his soda across the table. Cole put his spoon down, harder than he'd intended. No one spoke. They just turned to stare at him. Dammit, when she said it like that, it sounded terrible. Not at all like the sensible course he'd outlined. "It's more complicated than that."

She nodded. "Right. He also wants to pay me to be the child's mother, but only for a year or two, right, Cole?"

He should escort her to the door right now. Put an end to this before she caused any more havoc. Instead of answering her, he pushed back his chair and stood up. "I'm sure you gentlemen will excuse us. The lady and I have things to discuss."

Five chairs scraped, and five men tipped their hats in her direction before beating a hasty retreat. Half their ice cream lay melting in their bowls.

"That wasn't nice."

"I don't need to be nice. This is my ranch. We do things my way here."

"I know."

"We like it that way."

"Is that the royal *We?*"

His hands flexed in his desire to wring her pretty neck. Why the hell didn't she button her blouse properly? If she thought she'd get a reaction out of him, well...

She'd be right.

Dinner had been hell. He hadn't wanted a woman so much in years. Maybe ever. She made him furious, but she also made him hard. She'd be something in bed. A wild filly meant to be tamed.

But that wasn't the point. "Look, Ms. Garrett, I don't think—"

She got up from her chair and headed his way. He fought the urge to run, more worried about the look in her eyes than the sway of her hips. She moved real close. Near enough for him to get a whiff of her perfume.

"I know what you're going to say," she said, her voice softer than it had any reason to be. "You're going to say this isn't going to work. But I don't think you're right."

"No?"

Her mane of hair shimmered as she shook her head. "Something tells me I should stay. For a little while longer, at least. I feel this compelling need to understand what's going on here. Not just the fact that you want to do what you want to do, but that I'm considering doing it with you. That's a puzzle, don't you think?''

He wanted to smile. She'd given her speech with such seriousness, and shockingly enough, he'd understood her. But he was going to disappoint her. She wasn't the right woman for the job. Not at all.

''You're still thinking I'm not the right woman for the job, aren't you?''

He blinked at his own transparency. He'd trained himself never to give anything away by expression or posture. In fact, he'd probably have made a great poker player.

''It may turn out that I'm not,'' she went on. ''But I think we ought to wait a little longer. It's only the first day, after all. Besides, there's something you don't know about me.''

''What?''

''I'm a terrific cook.''

''We don't need a cook.''

She cocked an eyebrow. Even he couldn't let that lie stand. ''Okay. We do, but it's not going to be you.''

''Why not? I'm here. I need the work. The men need the nourishment.''

He looked at her long and hard. She didn't flinch, didn't blush. She was a piece of work, that's for sure. Her children would probably inherit that cocky attitude, that willingness to step up to the plate.

''All right,'' he said, knowing he was going to regret the decision. ''But just for a couple of days until I find a new full-time cook.''

She nodded. ''Good. I think that will give us plenty of time to decide if we want to have a baby together.''

She'd done it again. Made it sound foolish. But he knew better. His plan was a good one, dammit. It would give him everything he wanted. Well, almost everything.

CHAPTER SEVEN

LILY STOOD UP, feeling slightly less than triumphant. This was not easy. Cole was not easy. If only she could be certain things would work out the way she wanted them to. Eve had become a good friend, and in her heart Lily knew that whatever was ailing Mr. Granite would be helped by mending some old fences.

More than most people, Lily understood how important it was to nurture family connections. Her whole history—the Trueblood side of her family—was all about that. Reconciliation. Finding love when all seemed hopeless. It wasn't by accident that she and Dylan had come to form Finders Keepers. It was destiny. And bringing Cole and Eve together was destiny, too.

Cole folded his napkin and put it on the table. "Do you want to start tonight?"

"Start what?"

"Your cooking duties."

"Why, you didn't get enough to eat?"

He cocked his head slightly to the right. "I meant the clean up. Around here, if you cook, you clean."

She smiled. "Sorry, wrong answer, but thanks for playing."

"What?"

God, he was good-looking when he was bewildered. "I'll cook three meals a day, and I'll clean up after breakfast and lunch, but dinner is out of the question."

"Why?"

"Because I don't clean up after dinner."

His lips pressed together in a hard line for a few seconds, but then his shoulders relaxed. "Is there something wrong with you? Are you ill?"

"Nope."

"Is there some religious significance to the dinner meal?"

"Only on Christmas."

"And yet, you don't—"

"Clean up—"

"After dinner."

She nodded.

"I see. Then I'm afraid — "

"You know what my specialty is?" she said, interrupting him with the voice she used to get special favors. "Barbecued ribs that fall off the bone. Biscuits so light they practically float to the ceiling. And the best damn peach pie in five counties. No brag, just fact. And that's just for starters."

It worked. She could see it in his eyes. That he actually licked his lower lip was something of a clue, too, but the proof of the pudding was in his eyes. Sex and food. Men could be made to do practically anything for both, if used correctly. Why more women didn't utilize this potent combination, she wasn't sure. But growing up on a ranch with a whole herd of men around, she'd learned to cook early and well. As for the sex part? She could win a few blue ribbons at that, too, if she did say so herself.

"I'll make it easy on you," she said. "Call the guys. Let's see if they're willing to do it my way."

"You know they are. They'd build you a house if they thought it would mean three good squares a day."

"Then it's all settled."

"I don't like it."

She patted his hand. "I know, honey. But don't worry. It's all going to work out. I promise."

He didn't seem to believe her. Hell, she didn't know if she believed herself. But she wasn't about to stop now. She'd learned a few things in the FBI. First, if you wanted to get the job done, it was better to apologize later than ask permission now. Second, once a course was decided, it was vital to be committed and stay committed. It was the doubt that got you into hot water.

So she was going to be a cook, at least for a little while. About that, there had been no lies told. She was a great cook. She'd learned from her parents, both of whom were talented in the kitchen, and knew that good dishes came from the best ingredients. If J.T. had been doing the shopping as well as the cooking, she might be going to the store tonight.

Leaving Cole and his perpetual scowl, she went into the kitchen, prepared for an ungodly mess. But it wasn't bad at all. Good for J.T. Unfortunately, her luck didn't hold when she opened the fridge. Although she'd looked inside earlier when she'd gotten a soda, she hadn't been concerned with potential ingredients or lack thereof. There was a gallon of milk, three tubs of butter, and enough beer to sink a battleship. The vegetable crisper contained a bag of unopened mini carrots, the fruit bin was barren, and although there was meat in the freezer, she could hardly tell what it was for the freezer burn.

She closed the door and nearly leaped out of her skin to see Cole standing right there, only inches from her, a repeat of that afternoon. The man needed a bell around his neck. Well, around some part of his body. She grinned at the image, which seemed to upset him.

"What is that about?" he asked, meaning her smile. Maybe "growled" was more accurate.

"Nothing. I need to go shopping."

"When?"

"Before breakfast."

He snorted. Not a disgusting snort. Just one of those I knew all along this was going to be a pain in the ass snorts.

"You don't have to go with me," she said.

"No? Can you cover the cost?"

She could, with her trusty gold American Express card, but he didn't need to know that. "Well..."

"I thought not."

"You could always give me your credit card."

The look he gave her was what she expected. *Not in this lifetime, babe.*

"Have it your way," she said. "I'm ready when you are."

"I have to work tonight."

"Go right ahead. I'm sure no one will mind oatmeal tomorrow morning instead of the eggs, bacon and pancakes I was going to make."

He looked at her for another long minute, his granite facade not quite so solid, then turned on his heel and headed for the door.

"Excuse me."

He didn't stop.

"Excuse me!"

He paused at the door.

"Does this mean you'd like to go shopping now?" she asked.

"Yes."

"Okay. Only I have to get my purse. And make a list of the things we'll need. So you just wait right there." She headed toward the hallway, walking quickly past him toward her room.

"Ms. Garrett."

She didn't stop.

"Lily!"

That did it. She turned. Smiled sweetly. "Yes?"

"How long is this going to take?"

"The shopping? Or the getting ready to shop?"

"The getting ready."

"About half an hour."

"Tell you what. You do what you need to do, and I'll be in my office, waiting."

"Perfect."

As he walked away, she heard him sigh. She recognized the sound very well. She'd heard it all her life. From her father and Dylan to her professors and her bosses. Half the conversations she'd had since puberty had ended with the other party sighing. She used to take it personally. Not anymore. In fact, she was rather proud of her ability to confound. In this situation in particular it was wise to keep Cole Bishop off-balance. He was too darned used to being in control. She'd just have to see about that.

COLE HAD NEVER been keen on shopping. Not for clothes, not for gifts, not for anything. But of all the shopping he disliked, food shopping was the worst.

Lily, on the other hand, looked as if she was here for the duration. Her list in one hand, her pen in the other, she went aisle by slow aisle, with him being the good little houseboy, pushing the cart.

"I wonder if there's any whole wheat flour in the pantry. I forgot to look." She turned to him as if he'd know.

"I have no idea."

"You eat, don't you?"

"But I hire people to cook for me."

Her hands went to her hips and her brows lifted. "That's right. You do. So how much am I going to get?"

"Not a cent."

"No?"

"You volunteered, remember?"

"So that means it's not worth anything? Hogwash."

"I didn't say it wasn't worth—" Again, he stopped himself. He wasn't completely certain how she got to him like this, but she did. Consistently. Dammit, people were intimidated by him. Didn't she know that? Exasperating woman. Her child would probably inherit that lip. That sass. Who wanted a smart-aleck kid? Nobody, that's who.

His gaze went to the shopping cart. A big old leg of lamb stared up at him, and the thought of what J.T.—or any of the men—would do to that perfect piece of meat gave him pause. As soon as he found another cook, the situation would right itself. "I'll pay you a hundred a day."

"You'll pay me one hundred dollars?" Her voice seemed particularly loud in the cramped cereal aisle.

He looked at her again and felt a knot in his stomach at her satisfied grin. Damn it. She'd done it to him again. "Only if you're worth it."

"Oh, honey. For a hundred dollars a day, I'll make you and all the men so happy you won't know how to thank me."

Behind him, Cole heard a feminine gasp. He turned to see Julianne Roberts, the mayor's wife, staring at him, righteous indignation making her nostrils flare. It took him a second to realize what was up. That she'd overheard that last bit of conversation and gotten the wrong idea. "No," he began, "you don't understand...."

He reached out, but Mrs. Roberts jerked back. "Excuse me." Then she pushed her cart down the aisle so fast she knocked into a display of laundry detergent, starting an avalanche of blue boxes that spread into the pet food aisle.

"Hey, nice neighbors you got here."

Whirling on Lily, he froze her with a stare. "That was not amusing."

The left corner of Lily's lip curled up. "Actually, it was."

"You have a very sick sense of humor."

"Yeah. I know. But come on. Did you see her face? The way her nose was twitching, she looked like an indignant bunny rabbit."

Cole bit the inside of his cheek. The image, however, didn't disappear with the pain. He shifted his gaze to her hand. "What's next on the list?"

She shook her head and sighed, but didn't belabor the point. She just headed toward the produce section.

Cole stayed silent for the rest of the trip, despite the fact that Lily did everything under the sun to get a reaction from him. He remained stoic, silent, unflinching. Except when she wasn't looking. Then he cursed himself for the fool he was. For the trouble he had let himself in for. For the way he ached with wanting her.

LILY PUT the last of the vegetables in the crisper, then proceeded to fold the paper bags from the store. She'd had to explore a bit to find out where things were kept, but now she had the kitchen logistics down. She'd get the coffee ready tonight, and in the morning she'd make her mother's famous buttermilk pancakes. The men would be happy.

But that still left the rest of tonight to get through. It was only nine-thirty. Cole had retreated to his office, the coward. The rest of the men were already in the bunkhouse.

Maybe Cole would like something to drink. That would be a nice thing, wouldn't it? Considerate. He was probably thirsty by now.

Oh, dammit, she needed to lay off. Leave him be. If only the urge to needle him wasn't quite so powerful. But the way he struggled to keep his control was something to behold. She wanted him to laugh. Really laugh. The kind that cleansed the soul. She had a feeling he hadn't done that in a long, long time.

She sat down at the kitchen table, listening for signs of life. Nothing but the buzz of the fridge. Her thoughts went directly to this afternoon. When he'd kissed her. When he'd held all the cards, every one. And yet he'd pulled back.

It was a form of control, she understood that. Despite his denial, it had been a test, but *she* hadn't been the subject. The physical pull between them was real enough, but then, his whole plan was designed to eliminate such base urges. He didn't want to need anyone, not physically, not emotionally.

But that wasn't the whole story. Not that she was a psychologist or anything, but she knew something about human nature. And what she knew about Cole was that there was someone inside that fortress of his. Someone who wanted to be challenged, who wanted to laugh, and who wanted to care. The key to unleashing that part of him was getting him to connect to his past. He didn't know it, but she was going to save his life. By bringing him back to Eve, she would smash down the walls around his heart.

She hadn't made a conscious decision to be a smart-ass with him, but now that she thought about it, her instincts had been right on the money. He needed someone like her. Someone who didn't cower at that scowl of his.

This was going to work. She'd bring him back to his family, bring laughter into his brooding silence, get him to abandon this dumb idea to buy a kid. Dylan would say she was being a might optimistic, but she didn't think so.

She was here for a reason, and it wasn't just so Finders Keepers would earn its fee. She was here to do a much bigger job. After all, she was a Trueblood.

COLE TURNED OFF his computer and stared at the blank screen. He'd gotten nothing done. Well, except for stringing about fifty paper clips together. Which was crazy. This was the part of his work he liked. The books, the projections, the budgets. All the things a rancher was supposed to hate. Not him. He belonged at his desk—thinking, planning. But tonight, he'd been useless. Lily wouldn't leave him be.

Knowing she was just down the hall was torture. It didn't help when he told himself it was purely physical. That he wanted her because she was the most interesting and frustrating woman he'd met in years.

That was the problem. She was beautiful, strong, willful, determined and witty. All the things he appreciated in a woman. All the things that made him stop thinking clearly.

He truly didn't understand women. Yeah, lots of men said that, but in his case it was achingly true. They bewildered him, confused him, made him question himself. It was easier all the way around if he just avoided them, as if he were allergic to them. Oh, the occasional meeting didn't stir any symptoms, not even when that meeting was in the Jessup Motel. But long exposure wasn't smart.

He should tell her to leave. That would be safe. On the other hand, what man in his right mind wouldn't want her as the mother of his child? All those qualities of hers were exactly what he'd hoped for.

The other women he'd interviewed had shown him how rare it was to find someone like Lily. But would a woman like Lily really settle for the arrangement he had proposed?

Nice little paradox.

One he wasn't going to settle tonight. He turned off the computer, threw the paper clip chain in the top drawer and headed for the kitchen.

She wasn't there. Which was fine, except he'd wanted her to be. He'd actually found himself looking forward to sparring with her. Yet another warning sign.

He got himself a Corona and unscrewed the cap. It was nearly eleven, and he liked to get to sleep before midnight so he could start the day early. No way was he going to fall asleep anytime soon. Not when he was keyed up like this.

He took a long drink, then headed out for the back porch. It was still hot—this was Texas after all—but comforting in an odd way. The sultry air carried the scent of night-blooming jasmine, a smell that reminded him of his first girlfriend. He'd been fifteen, and she'd been fourteen, and he used to sneak out of his bedroom window in the middle of the night and run to her house, where she'd be waiting in the garden. They'd kissed. Not very well, actually. He hadn't heard of French kissing back then, and neither had she. But the passion in those closed-mouth clinches had been undeniable.

His gaze moved up to the sky and a million stars. Cicadas sang a loud chorus, and still Cole couldn't relax. He'd never been what you could call laid-back, but in the last few years, especially since he'd decided on his future, he'd found some respite. If she stayed, he probably wouldn't feel calm again. Not until she left. Could he tolerate a couple of years of this tension? For himself, no. But was anything too much to ask for his child?

"Are you going to speak to me or just howl at the moon?"

Cole jerked back, nearly dropping his beer. He found her sitting on the chair, alone on the porch. She seemed to meld with the night, be part of it. Even now that he knew she was there, she wasn't easy to see.

"Didn't mean to scare you."

"I didn't know you were out here."

"It's okay. I wasn't sure whether to stay quiet or

not. You looked like you were pretty deep in thought. But then, I figured if you tried to sit down, you'd probably have a coronary or something, and I haven't brushed up on my CPR lately.''

"Thanks. I think."

"I'd offer you a chair, but there isn't one."

"I've been meaning to get some."

"Yeah. Ruling an empire is hell."

He was glad it was so dark. He didn't want her to see his smile. No use making her any cockier than she already was.

"Hey, Cole?"

"Yes?"

"Now that I'm an employee and all, why don't you tell me something about yourself."

"I don't like talking about myself."

"Do you have something to hide?"

He hesitated. Not because he didn't want to answer her, but because he didn't necessarily want to give her his usual answer. If things were going to work out between them, if she was going to be the mother of his kid, she had a right to know some things. Not everything. But some.

"You're not an ax murderer or anything, are you?"

"No."

"So what's the big deal? Everybody has a lousy past. Everybody has stuff they regret. It doesn't mean anything unless you let it."

He bristled at the pop psychology. What she considered lousy and he considered lousy were two very different things. "There are no medical risks, I promise you that."

"Nope. Not good enough."

"What is it you need to know?"

She stood, walked over to him. "You stay right there. Don't move." Then she hurried into the house.

A few moments later, she came out holding one of the dining room chairs. She set it down opposite the old wooden porch rocker, then took her place once more. "Sit."

"I—"

"Oh, don't give me excuses, just sit for heaven's sake."

He opened his mouth, then realized he really had only two choices. Sit, or go inside. Inside was safe. But outside had Lily. He walked over to the chair and sat, his knees just a couple of inches from her.

"Thank you." She patted his knee, a perfectly innocent gesture that made his pulse go crazy.

"Now we can talk. What I want to know about is you. Where you grew up, what you were like as a kid, what brought you to this place in your life."

"There's really no need for you to know all that."

"Yes, there is."

"Why? I told you all the important details. There's no medical risk. No criminal past. Nothing that would have an impact on you getting pregnant."

"But I need to know."

"Why?"

Her head tilted slightly, but he couldn't see the details of her face. Or her eyes. "Because it matters. If you're serious about this, and I think you are, you must know there's an inherent flaw in your plan. You want a mother's love to help mold and shape your child, but the child isn't going to want to stop being loved just because the timer goes off. You may be able to have a marriage that's a business arrangement. Of that, I'm pretty sure. It can work, too. I think it happens more often than anyone thinks. But the kid issue is something else entirely.''

''You don't understand.''

''Then help me. Tell me about you, Cole. Let me understand.''

He almost said no. He'd tried like hell to forget his past. But her words had a ring of truth to them, even though he wasn't about to alter his plan now. For his son's sake, he'd talk.

CHAPTER EIGHT

LILY DIDN'T press him. In fact, she remained completely still, hardly daring to breathe. It was like being inches from a wild buck who could bolt at any second.

She wished she could see him more clearly. The stars were bright, but the moon was a crescent. His body language told her several things. His arms were relaxed, not folded across his chest or anything, yet he had one hell of a grip on his beer bottle. He leaned slightly forward, which was an indication that he was willing to share, but he wouldn't look at her.

As the seconds ticked by, she marveled at her own audacity. She'd met this man today, and here she was asking him to share his secrets. Yet it made its own kind of sense. Something she'd learned in her years in law enforcement was that most folks will reveal more to a total stranger than someone in their immediate circle, especially if what they had to say was painful. Why that should be so, she didn't know, but she'd seen it time and time again.

She'd discussed it once with a professor, and he'd theorized that the need to talk, to unburden, was hardwired—one of the ways human beings stayed connected as part of a community. But such honesty also made us vulnerable, so it was better to let it all out with someone who could do you no harm.

Cole's gaze was on her. She didn't remember him looking up, but he must have when she was so lost in thought. His expression, what she could see of it, didn't seem terribly open. Oh, well. It had been worth a shot. Maybe in a day or so, she'd try again. See if she could get him to trust her a little more.

She started to get up, but stopped when he cleared his throat.

"I was raised in San Antonio. In the King William district. My parents married too young. My mother was only sixteen, and my father was eighteen. I was born shortly after the wedding. We lived with my grandparents for a long time."

"Your father's parents?"

He nodded. "They had this huge place, with acres of land. I was an only child, but I was never bored. There was always something to do, and my mother was almost a playmate."

He took a long drink from his beer, then leaned forward so his elbows were on his thighs. "My father was gone a lot. He traveled for business. I worshipped him. He used to bring me things from all over the world. One time it was an electric scooter from Germany. Camping gear from Alaska. A kite from Japan. But I didn't see him very often."

"That must have been hard."

"It was okay. I got along fine. My mother was there. And we took care of each other. She had no one. Her parents had died when she was four, and she'd been raised by her aunt. But her aunt had gone into a home the year before my mother and father met."

"Oh, my. She must have doted on you."

He nodded. "For a while."

"What do you mean?"

He stood up and walked over to the railing, where he leaned forward, staring into the darkness. "There was this Saturday I was supposed to go to a basketball game with my dad. We had our own place by then. The Spurs were playing that day, and I was a huge fan. Only, my dad couldn't make it. He said he had to work. My mom saw how disappointed I was, and she ended up taking me, even though she didn't like sports. During the second quarter, the camera scanned the crowd, you know, where the pictures come up on the giant screen. And there was my father. He had his arm around this woman's shoulders, and she was laughing and she buried her head in his neck when she saw the camera was on them. And then, this kid— he was about my age at the time—climbed up on my dad's lap and waved. Like *he* was his son, not me."

"Who were they?"

"I didn't know for a long time. My mother took me to my grandmother's for a while. I didn't see either of my parents for almost a month. But then my mother came and got me. Everything had changed. She wasn't the same anymore. My father never talked about that woman or that kid. Finally, when I was about fifteen, I found out that the woman was his mistress and the boy was his son. My half brother."

"Did you discuss it with your father?"

"Nope. And I never met them, either. Never even tried."

"What a jackass."

Cole turned. "Excuse me?"

"Not you. Your father. He was a jerk."

Cole smiled. She could see it clearly, even in the dim moonlight. "Yeah. He was."

"But your grandmother. She was there for you, wasn't she? She took care of you?"

He nodded as he walked back to the chair. He didn't sit, though. He just put one of his strong hands on the back. "She did. She made sure I had everything. A good education, a car when I got my driver's license."

"But...?"

He opened his mouth, but only to finish off his beer. When he brought the bottle down, he shrugged slightly. "It's late. It's been a long day."

"That it has." She stood, wanting to move closer to him. Knowing it wasn't the time. "When does everyone show up for breakfast?"

"Six-thirty."

"It'll be ready."

"You have everything you need in your room?"

"Yep."

"Okay, then."

She smiled.

He didn't move. He just stood there.

"Is there something else?" she asked, taking a tentative step toward him.

"No. It's just that—"

"What?"

"I haven't thought about some things for a long time."

"I didn't mean to stir up bad memories."

"That's just it. I'm remembering some good things, too. My mom was real pretty. And she had the nicest voice. She used to sing me Beatles' songs. And she had this yellow dress."

"Where is she now?"

"She died eleven years ago."

"I'm sorry."

"Yeah. Me, too." With that, he walked to the porch steps and headed off somewhere, maybe the barn. Maybe just a private place.

It was time to turn in. She just hoped she could get some sleep. There was so much to think about. Not the least of which was the way she wanted to comfort him. To hold him, pet his hair, tell him it was going to be all right.

It was kind of scary, when she got right down to it. She wasn't supposed to feel anything for him. He was a case, that's all. She needed to be objective. Impartial.

Man, was she in trouble.

DYLAN GLANCED at the clock and winced at the hour. It was nearly 4:00 a.m., so what in hell was he doing in his office? Torturing himself, that's what. He'd pulled out an old box of letters, one he hadn't even known he'd saved. In fact, he had a suspicion *he* hadn't been the one to stow them. The box had Lily's fingerprints all over it. She was a firm believer in the written word, and it was beyond her why everyone in the world didn't keep a journal.

He never was that comfortable with a pen, or even a keyboard. It felt too risky to write about the real stuff. But there had been a few years when he'd followed Lily's example. Only he hadn't written in a diary. He'd written to Julie.

The top envelope was made out to him. Julie's pretty handwriting was as familiar to him as his own. He pulled the note from inside and looked at the date.

March 18, 1989. He hadn't known her long. But he'd already fallen in love with her. The part he couldn't recall was whether he'd admitted the fact to himself at that point. Probably not. He wasn't the brightest kid on the block when it came to matters of the heart.

Dear Dylan,

If I get through economics without killing myself, we'll have to celebrate. Maybe pizza and a bottle of wine? But none of those awful anchovies! Did I tell you I put your buckle on the wall? I even framed it. The other girls in the dorm are all jealous, and oh, Carol Lacey really likes you and wants to ask you out. But I just love the way the buckle shines, and I'm so proud of you for winning at the national rodeo! I know Sebastian was green with envy. But that's okay. He'll get over it. He wants us to go see *Batman*, but I just can't picture Michael Keaton in it, can you? I do like Jack Nicholson, though. Will you come with us? I have a little secret to tell you. I had a dream about you last night. It was, well, it was pretty risqué.

He crumpled the paper in his hand, unable to read another word. She'd dreamed about him once. She'd lived in his dreams, coming to him again and again, only in his dreams she loved him, which was the cruelest part of all. Because he'd wake up every morning and remember it wasn't true.

She was still alive. He knew it with absolute certainty. Something would have died inside him if she wasn't. But where was she? *Where?*

COLE TURNED OVER and punched his pillow, trying to find a comfortable position. It was past four, and he'd only slept in bits and snatches, awakened time and again by nightmares. Not about monsters or falling into dark voids or things that go bump in the night. His nightmares were all about one thing—Lily.

She'd done something to him. Put a hex or a curse on his head. He never talked about his family. Not to anyone. Not even his closest friends.

Huh. His closest friends were Chigger and Manny. There was no one from the old days, from his past. And he wanted it that way. For him, everything that had come before the ranch was dead and buried. His real life had started five years ago.

So why had he dredged up those memories tonight? Just because she'd asked? That was ridiculous. And true.

Dammit, why was this so complicated? If he'd been a woman, he could have gotten pregnant any damn time he wanted, and that would have been that. The father wouldn't have had to know a thing. So why in hell didn't he just adopt?

He turned over, his sleep-deprived brain cutting right to the chase. His ego, that's why. He had no desire to raise some other man's child. He wanted this done his way.

Lily had a lot of things going for her. But she had even more against. No way could they go through with this. He wouldn't be able to keep his hands off her. Not that he would do anything against her will, but there was no denying the two of them had chemistry.

She'd be a pain. She'd want to be part of his son's life forever. She'd drive him crazy.

She already had.

If only she didn't have that hair. Or those legs, or that mouth, or those eyes... Hell, it was the package that appealed, not the parts.

She was something. Sassy and bright, infuriating and intriguing. But then, he didn't really know her, did he? He'd proven to himself that he wasn't a good judge of women, so why was he jumping to conclusions now? He had a feeling it had more to do with sex than with wisdom.

He ached from want. All the way to his bones. And she was the cure.

Okay, so maybe she wasn't the right woman for the job, but maybe she could be right in another way. Maybe she'd be amenable to a different kind of arrangement. One that didn't have lasting repercussions.

He sighed, wishing he could turn off his thoughts and get to sleep. Tomorrow would be hell. He wasn't one who could go without sleep easily. Not like Chigger, who only needed about four hours a night.

The best thing to do was just forget about her and think of something else. Work. Right. That journalist for *The Cattlemen* was coming tomorrow. No, not for a couple of days. Dammit, he didn't even know what day it was. All because of her.

WORD MUST have gotten around. It was the only explanation she could come up with. The hands arrived a little after six. No one she knew on a ranch ever got up earlier than they needed to. Thank goodness the coffee was ready. The men, after asking if there was anything she needed them for, were at the dining room table drinking coffee, lying through their teeth and laughing it up.

All except Cole.

Lily tested the griddle. The temperature was perfect, and she ladled out the first batch of hotcakes. The big pan of scrambled eggs would be ready at the same time, as would the bacon. She had the feeling there wouldn't be any leftovers.

As she cooked, she wondered about the rest of the day. Of course, there were two more meals to prepare, but that wasn't going to take all her time. She'd like to go for a ride, if Cole would lend her a horse. She'd also like to nap and catch up on the sleep she'd missed last night.

Normally, she slept like a baby anywhere. Nothing fazed her. Except thoughts of this case. And Cole. She'd ended up turning on the light at three and scribbling in her journal. Unfortunately, all she'd written were questions, no answers. What was it about him that made her so…itchy? And why in hell did she want him to scratch that itch when she knew perfectly well that it was completely inappropriate and stupid?

She was on the rebound, which accounted for a lot, but not all. Something else was at work here. Unfortunately, she had no idea what.

She turned the pancakes, and for the next fifteen minutes concentrated on nothing but the meal. When it was done, she went to the kitchen door and called for a little help. Of course, the first one she looked for was Cole, but his seat was still empty. All the other guys jumped up, which was sweet. She nodded at Spence and Manny. They helped her carry the food to the table.

Everything looked great. And smelled better. She'd even brought out another pot of coffee and a pitcher of orange juice. So why was everyone sitting there with empty plates in front of them?

"Uh, guys? Is there a problem?"

Chigger cleared his throat. "No, ma'am. We're just waiting for you."

"Well, don't. I'll be there shortly. You guys just eat."

That was all it took. They attacked the food like ravenous hyenas. No more talk. No more laughter. Just the sound of utensils hitting plates.

She was no Emeril, but the yummy sounds coming from the men made her feel like a master chef. Her pleasure wasn't complete, however. The boss was still missing in action.

Chigger swallowed some orange juice then turned to her. "Ms. Lily?"

"Yes?"

"If you'll pardon my language, this is the best damn meal we've had in ages."

She waved her hand at him. "Aw, shucks. If you think this is good, wait till dinner."

"I don't know that I'll be able to think of anything else."

"You'd better." Cole's voice came from the hallway.

Lily turned to see him walking toward her and her whole being reacted. Her heart squeezed, her pulse jumped, her skin tingled with goose bumps. It was entirely unsettling, and not a little annoying. What was it about him?

"Boss, you're just in time." Manny placed the bowl of eggs in front of Cole's place setting. There were some left, but not enough for seconds. "It was all we could do not to finish it off."

Cole pulled his chair back, his gaze darting to Lily,

then away. "Yeah, well, I had things to do this morning."

Chigger gave her a look that told her Cole was full of beans.

As Cole filled his plate, Lily reached for the pancakes. "I'll go heat these up."

He put his hand on hers, and it was as if she'd been hit by lightning. She nearly dropped the plate. He pulled away instantly, as if he'd been burned, too.

"Don't bother," he said, but his voice was grainy and stiff.

"It's no bother."

He finally looked at her. The contact made her knees weak. This was nuts. It wasn't possible. She didn't know him, she wasn't interested in getting to know him, except for Eve's sake, and she'd made a personal commitment to keep herself man-free for a year.

"Put the plate down, Lily."

His voice was clear again. That smooth, velvet tone swirled inside her head. She obeyed him, not because of his words, but because of the unsteadying effect his voice had on her.

She sat and picked up her fork, although the last thing on earth she wanted was food. But she couldn't just stare at him. She certainly couldn't lunge at him, although the thought of clearing the table with one sweep of her arm and going for it was highly appealing.

He hadn't eaten anything yet, either. His hair was still damp from the shower. His eyes seemed tired, but piercing nonetheless. It wasn't fair for him to be so good-looking. Although she knew her feelings weren't about his looks. Well, not entirely. This, she was afraid, was chemistry. Or would that be biology?

Cole jerked his gaze away and shoved a forkful of food in his mouth.

As he did, she pulled herself together. It took all her will, and all her concentration. So that was probably why she hadn't realized she and Cole were alone. That all the men had disappeared. She hadn't heard a sound.

This was not good.

CHAPTER NINE

DYLAN PICKED UP the phone on the third ring.

"It's me."

He bit back a sigh of disappointment. He'd been expecting a call from an informant about a certain carjacker. But his sister didn't call all that often, so something must be up. "Hey, Ashley. What's wrong?"

"Nothing. Just checking in. Have you heard from Lily?"

"Not today."

"Oh."

"Ash?"

"Yeah?"

"Come on. Spill."

Her sigh traveled over the phone line so clearly he could see her expression in his mind's eye. She'd be leaning back in her chair, head tilted to the side, her mouth in the pout she'd used well since birth. "Out with it."

"It's a client."

"Uh-oh." Ashley worked as a junior account executive with a San Antonio based advertising agency and seemed to have more than her share of problems with male clients.

"I know. Can you stand it? It happened again."

"Is he married?"

"Seven years, and he has two kids. Honestly, Dylan, I don't get it. I don't encourage them at all. Not even a little."

"Oh?"

"Well, maybe I flirt a little. But that's innocent stuff, and anyone would have to be a dope not to realize it."

"So this client is a dope?"

"Yeah, but a rich dope."

"That makes things a little more complicated."

"I know. I really do want his business. I just want him to get any other ideas out of his head."

"You've done it before."

She sighed again. "Maybe it is me. Maybe I'm asking for trouble and I don't even see it."

"Ashley, honey, you're a beautiful woman. You could stand perfectly still and not say one word, and men would still try their best with you."

"I swear, men just make things so complicated."

"Not all men."

"I'd like to meet one who doesn't."

"Me?"

"Nope. You make things complicated, too."

"Hey."

"Come on, big brother. I lived with you for a long time. I know about you and—" She cut off her sentence.

"About me and?"

"Nothing."

"Julie. Is that what you were going to say?"

"Yeah. But that's because my mouth was in gear while my brain wasn't. I'm sorry."

"It's okay. It was true. But now all I want is to see her safe."

"I know, Dylan. Listen, I gotta run, but I love you. And say hi to Lily for me, okay?"

"You got it."

"Dylan?"

"Yeah?"

"Are you all right?"

"I'm fine. Honest."

"Okay. Talk to you soon."

He hung up the phone, wondering if everyone in his family knew about his feelings for Julie. Of course Lily did, but he'd never suspected Ashley had a clue. Great. So they were all probably feeling sorry for him. That was just perfect.

He sat down, looked at her picture, and shook his head. "Where are you?"

DINNER WAS another triumph for Lily. She'd made prime rib, scalloped potatoes, asparagus in brown butter, rolls and her famous peach pie for dessert. The praise made her blush, and secretly wonder if she should have gone to the Culinary Institute of America instead of the Federal Bureau of Investigation.

The only thorn in the crown was Cole. He'd disappeared shortly after breakfast, hadn't joined the rest of the crew for lunch, and when he finally came in for dinner, he was markedly silent and sullen.

She had seen him once, though. She'd been in the kitchen, washing glasses, and she'd caught a movement out of the corner of her eye. Cole. He was by the porch, not on it. And he'd been looking right at her.

She'd thought he would bolt as soon as she met his gaze, but he didn't. He stared at her in a way that made her heat with a blush. It wasn't a sexual thing.

Well, not entirely. It was blatant hunger, and something more. Something that frightened her. Before she could figure it out, he'd turned and walked away.

She'd watched him until he passed out of sight. His straight back, the way he held himself...so proud. It was nuts how she felt about him. As if he needed her. As if she had been brought here for him, not Eve.

He'd never left her thoughts for the rest of the day. And now he sat at the table, quiet, drawn inside himself. There was a fortress around him, and she had no idea how to get inside.

When she'd asked Chigger if he knew what was wrong, the old man had been just as bewildered. He'd said something interesting, however. "Don't you pay no mind to his moodiness. Cole Bishop is one of the finest men I've ever met, and if he's on your side, you'll never have to be scared."

All through dessert she'd thought about that comment. If she trusted Chigger's assessment, then she had little to worry about. Cole would eventually come around. But sometimes friends had blind spots. Perhaps Chigger wanted his boss to be a fine man, and forgave the evidence that he wasn't.

The thing was, she needed to spend more time with Cole. Staying in the house all day while he worked outside wasn't exactly going to get the job done. So tonight, she'd have to make up for lost time. Shake him out of his sullen mood and get him talking.

Cole didn't say his first word to her until he finished the last of his pie. "Thanks." The single word came with a short nod of the head, as impersonal as he could get without just putting a buck on the table. Then he got up and walked down the hallway, his back straight, his shoulders so wide she thought they might touch the walls.

"I sure wish Cole would learn to shut up," Manny said. "Man can talk your ear off."

The others laughed, and she smiled with them, but her preoccupation was such that she hardly registered that they were all looking at her, and that other than the one comment, the lively chatter of a few moments ago had come to a halt.

"Why don't you go on, Ms. Lily," Chigger said in a sort of stage whisper. "We've got dishes to do."

She nodded, touched his shoulder as she got up. Then she walked toward the back of the house to find Cole Bishop.

He was in the last place she looked. The nursery. He wasn't doing anything, simply standing in the room, his arms folded across his chest, his gaze on the empty crib. She knocked, but he didn't acknowledge her. Perhaps he didn't hear her. She stepped inside the room as quietly as she could, torn between pushing him and leaving him to his private thoughts.

For a long time, they both stood silently, Lily leaning against the door watching him. His chest rose and fell rhythmically, almost as if he were asleep. Perhaps he was in some sort of trance. Truly lost in thought. About what? The child he wanted so desperately? The decision he'd made to have that child in such an unorthodox manner?

How she yearned to help him. To bring him solace. Why, she had no idea. A reaction to her own recent pain? A distraction from her own problems? Whatever the reason, it was as real as her heartbeat, and tangible as the door she leaned against.

His childhood, at least the tiny slice she knew of

it, wasn't enough of an explanation for the angst she saw in him. One event, even as hurtful as being betrayed by his father, wouldn't lead to this extreme. What else had occurred? Something to do with Eve, she felt sure. Something tragic, she feared.

"The dinner was a fine one."

His voice startled her, his words threw her off-balance. Dinner felt like a hundred years ago. "Thank you."

"The guys are pleased. But don't worry. You won't have to be here long. I called the agency. They'll start sending out applicants tomorrow or the next day."

"I'm not worried. Besides, I'd want to stay even if you did have a decent cook. This is a trial, remember? To see if you and I—"

He turned on her abruptly, as if he meant to scare her. Or hurt her. Her body tensed, ready to protect herself using whatever means necessary. But he stayed his ground. The only weapon he had was his eyes. The fire in them. But the heat wasn't just about this thing between them. This chemistry. There was anger in his gaze. Accusation.

"Why are you looking at me like that?" she asked.

"Because I don't know who you are or what you want."

"I told you—"

"How do I know you're telling me the truth?"

She blanched. Had he found out about her arrangement with Eve? About her true purpose in coming here?

"For all I know, you could be a scam artist out to steal my money, my land."

She let out a pent-up breath. Her real secret was safe. "I'm not."

"Oh, okay," he said sarcastically. "That convinces me."

"What brought this on? Last night—"

"Last night was nothing." His arms went to his sides and he took a step toward her. "It was a mistake."

"How could talking honestly be a mistake?"

His answer was in his icy stare.

"No matter what you think, I'm not the enemy."

His lips curled into a smile that was no smile at all but a dangerous mask, hiding a rage that simmered just below the surface. "You are. You're everything I'm afraid of."

Despite a shiver of fear, she stepped closer to him. "Why? Why me?"

"You're a— You're after something. Don't tell me you're not."

"Okay. I won't deny it. I am after something."

"I knew it," he said, the words ground out like broken glass.

She almost told him everything. That she was a private investigator, and that she was here to bring him back to his family before it was too late. But then she remembered Eve's face—the desperation and need for this woman to make amends. How could she betray her friend? She hated the lies, but she knew without a doubt that she was doing a good thing. That Cole would thank her in the end.

His right brow rose, urging her to talk.

"Shockingly enough, what I want has more to do with me than you. I'm here about a job. About a chance to change things for the better. And you're not making it very easy.''

His mouth had became a slim, hard line as his lips pressed together tightly. The suspicion in his gaze deepened.

"Why are you doing this, Cole? Why are you so angry? I don't mean just now. I can't understand why you'd be so angry at the world that you need to buy your own child."

"It's none of your goddamn business."

"Okay, fine. It's none of my business. But it's going to be someone's business, unless you want the mother of your child to be a moron. The question is legitimate."

"You want a legitimate question? Why are *you* here? You can have any man, and you know it. You don't need this arrangement. All you have to do is snap your fingers."

"Is that so?"

"You know it is."

"I don't know what planet you're from, but down here on earth, I'm no femme fatale. I'm thirty, and I've never had an honest relationship. The last man I was with, oh, he was something. He treated me like a queen, bought me presents, convinced me to move to a different city, get a job I wasn't even sure I wanted. He gave me a gorgeous engagement ring. We picked out a damn china pattern. After all that, after giving him everything, after building my dreams around him, I found out he was married. With two adorable children and a house in the suburbs. Oh, and that ring? As fake as he was."

Cole winced. A subtle movement she would have missed if she hadn't been staring at him so intently.

"You're not the only person who's ever had his heart broken," she assured him.

"How do you know I had my—" He stopped, closed his eyes for a moment.

"It's damn clear that you're hurting. But it's also clear you're an intelligent man. You have to know that you can't buy someone's love."

"I'm not trying to. I told you. The marriage would be in name only."

"Cole, that's not what I meant. You can't force a child to love you. It doesn't work that way."

"I won't have to force him. I'll give him everything."

"I don't see that you lacked for anything growing up. Did that work?"

"You don't know what you're talking about."

"No? Then tell me. Explain it to me."

He started to walk out, to leave her without explanation, but as he passed her, she touched his arm. She felt his muscle bunch under his shirt, felt his heat. He turned to her, and his gaze burned her once more.

"You need to go."

"All right. I will. But tell me why. Tell me what horrible sin I've committed."

His gaze raked her face. A second later, he'd broken her hold, and it was his hands on her arms. He held her tightly, hurting her. The power she'd seen in him from the first moment scared her now. She felt as if he could crush her. Instead, he kissed her.

He kissed her with all the pain and rage in his heart. Kissed her as if he could kill her with his lips.

She whimpered, and he flew back, releasing her, the shock on his face evidence enough that he hadn't meant her harm. The way he looked at her was more than she could stand. Such confusion, such need. He was drowning, right there in front of her. Drowning in a sorrow she could barely understand.

She touched his face, her palm against his cheek. He stood perfectly still, although she felt his jaw tense. "Who hurt you like this?"

"Don't."

"Don't what? Don't ask? Don't care?"

"That's right. Don't care."

She rose on her tiptoes. "Too late," she whispered. And then she kissed him. Gently. Willing him to feel her compassion. Urging him to take comfort.

His hard shoulders relaxed as he moaned, as his hands moved to pull her closer. She caressed his cheek, his hair. It was a moment of surrender, and not just on his part. Her awareness shifted as she tasted him, as his tongue slipped inside her. This was no act. She wasn't pretending. She needed to understand him. She'd known him two days and it felt like a lifetime. As if the want had always been inside her, dormant until he touched her.

He'd awakened something inside her. What she didn't know was if it would heal her, or break her.

CHAPTER TEN

COLE DRANK HER IN, her scent, her taste, the feel of her body against his. He wanted more. He wanted all of her.

She touched his tongue with hers, and he moaned as much in pain as in pleasure. If she knew what she was doing to him, she'd run as far and as fast as she could go. The urge to punish her for another's sins was almost as strong as his desire to take her. He had to hold on to the part of him that was sane, that told him she wasn't Carrie.

Her hand moved to the back of his neck, and her cool fingers made him tremble. He pressed himself against her, letting her feel his erection, showing her exactly what her touch was leading to.

Instead of pushing him away, she moved her hips.

He tore his lips from hers. "Get out of here, Lily. Get out before it's too late."

Her answer was to pull his head down and quiet him with another kiss.

There was no more strength to fight her. He moved with her until the door was at her back, and then he pressed his hips against her, put his hand on her breast. The feel of that softness beneath him made him hungrier still. Her nipple against his palm was as hard and stiff as he was, even through her shirt and bra.

GET 2

HOW TO GET YOUR
2 FREE BOOKS AND FREE GIFT!

1. Peel off the MIRA sticker on the front cover. Place it in the space provided at right. This automatically entitles you to receive two free books and an exciting mystery gift.

2. Send back this card and you'll get 2 "The Best of the Best™" novels. These books have a combined cover price of $11.00 or more in the U.S. and $13.00 or more in Canada, but they are yours to keep absolutely FREE!

3. There's <u>no</u> catch. You're under <u>no</u> obligation to buy anything. We charge nothing – ZERO – for your first shipment. And you don't have to make any minimum number of purchases – not even one!

4. We call this line "The Best of the Best" because each month you'll receive the best books by some of today's hottest authors. These authors show up time and time again on all the major bestseller lists and their books sell out as soon as they hit the stores. You'll like the convenience of getting them delivered to your home at our special discount prices . . . and you'll love your *Heart to Heart* subscriber newsletter featuring author news, horoscopes, recipes, book reviews and much more!

SPECIAL FREE GIFT!

We'll send you a fabulous surprise gift, absolutely FREE, simply for accepting our no-risk offer!

5. We hope that after receiving your free books you'll want to remain a subscriber. But the choice is yours – to continue or cancel, anytime at all! So why not take us up on our invitation, with no risk of any kind. You'll be glad you did!

6. And remember…we'll send you a mystery gift ABSOLUTELY FREE just for giving "The Best of the Best" a try.

Visit us online at
www.mirabooks.com

® and TM are trademarks of Harlequin Enterprises Limited.

BOOKS FREE!

Hurry!

Return this card
promptly to
**GET 2 FREE
BOOKS &
A FREE GIFT!**

The Best of the Best ™

YES! Please send me the 2 FREE "The Best of the Best" novels and FREE gift for which I qualify. I understand that I am under no obligation to purchase anything further, as explained on the opposite page.

(P-BB3-01)

385 MDL C6PQ   **185 MDL C6PP**

NAME   (PLEASE PRINT CLEARLY)

ADDRESS

APT.#   CITY

STATE/PROV.   ZIP/POSTAL CODE

▼ DETACH AND MAIL CARD TODAY! ▼

The Best of the Best™ — Here's How it Works:

Accepting your 2 free books and gift places you under no obligation to buy anything. You may keep the books and gift and return the shipping statement marked "cancel." If you do not cancel, about a month later we will send you 4 additional novels and bill you just $4.24 each in the U.S., or $4.74 each in Canada, plus 25¢ shipping & handling per book and applicable taxes if any.* That's the complete price and — compared to cover prices of $5.50 or more each in the U.S. and $6.50 or more each in Canada — it's quite a bargain! You may cancel at any time, but if you choose to continue, every month we'll send you 4 more books, which you may either purchase at the discount price or return to us and cancel your subscription.

*Terms and prices subject to change without notice. Sales tax applicable in N.Y. Canadian residents will be charged applicable provincial taxes and GST.

Leaving her lips, he dipped his head to her neck, to the hollow beneath her ear. He kissed her, nipped her, all the while showing her what he wanted with his body and his fingers.

"Cole." Her breath came out in a sultry whisper. "Cole, wait."

It was only then that he felt her hand against his chest. He lifted his head.

"We can't do this. It's not what either of us wants."

"Speak for yourself," he said, his voice a growl he barely recognized.

She moved to the side, away from him, and he lowered his gaze to her chest. To the stark evidence that he wasn't the only one wanting.

She blushed, which was something to behold. It caused her face to glow with an innocence that made him ache for her even more.

"Someone has to be sensible here," she said. "Sleeping together isn't going to help."

"You're wrong."

"No I'm not. It's a way to escape. To avoid the real issues."

"There are no issues."

"Right." The word hung in the air, flat, filled with disappointment. She turned and opened the door. "I'll get packed and be out of here within the hour."

He stopped her with his hand on her arm. "You don't have to go tonight."

"No?" She met his gaze. "What are you saying?"

He should tell her she could stay until morning. Get a good night's sleep before her long drive. That would solve his problem. He could go back to his comfortable life. He'd continue his search for a more suitable woman. For someone who wouldn't make him need or feel or care. "Stay..." The rest of the words wouldn't come. Because the thought of her leaving was just as upsetting as keeping her here.

"The night? Until you have a new cook? What?"

"I don't know. But we can figure it out tomorrow."

She looked at him for a long moment, then nodded. "All right."

"Lily..."

"Yes?"

He wanted to tell her that he couldn't stop thinking about her. That this spell she'd put him under was pure hell. That he'd never wanted anything as much as he wanted her in his bed. Instead, he said, "Nothing."

Her lips curved into a sad smile. "I think I'll turn in now. I'm pretty tired."

He nodded as he released her arm. The moment she was out the door, he wanted her back. What the hell was going on here? The whole day he'd thought about why she was the wrong one. About why she should leave. He had a hundred reasons. Was it her kiss that made him stupid? That made logic fly out the window?

Maybe he should go to Jessup. See if Noreen was busy tonight. That would help. Or would that only make him want Lily more? *Shit*. It was all wrong. All of it. But he wasn't willing to give up his plan. He *couldn't* trust Lily. If he did, he'd be a fool. Wanting her like this made him vulnerable, though. She could get to him with her body, just like Carrie had. And then he'd be right back where he'd started.

The best decision he'd ever made was to go solo.

To build his own unique family. To eliminate the danger of another woman ruining his life.

So why did he want Lily to stay? Was it just about sex? Or was something far more insidious going on? He leaned his forehead against the cool wood of the door. That was the problem, wasn't it? He had no idea if Lily was telling him the truth or not. He just couldn't see. It was like color blindness, only his problem was woman blindness. The only way to protect himself was to stay away. To send her away.

Tomorrow. Tomorrow, he'd tell her to go.

IN SAN ANTONIO, in a little bar that smelled faintly of wet dog, Sebastian Cooper sat in the darkest corner, milking a vodka rocks as he listened to Bob Seger and the Silver Bullet Band sing about old time rock and roll. In front of him, by the scratched, dirty pool table, a woman prepared to take her turn at eight ball.

She was in her thirties, and the years hadn't been kind. Her blond hair, piled up on her head, looked dry and brittle, especially under the harsh lights illuminating the green felt playing surface. She was the kind of thin that women liked to think was attractive, but most men found unappealing. She seemed all sharp edges instead of soft curves. Her clothes were too short, too small, too vulgar. When she laughed, which was often, she inevitably broke into a fit of coughing.

Her companion, an older woman who provided the hilarity, wore a T-shirt with the pithy slogan, *One tequila, Two tequila, Three tequila, Floor.* Her bons mots were well peppered with curses, one word in particular.

Both women stared at him. The younger with a lusty, if mercenary, gleam, the older through a drunken haze.

Sebastian took another sip of the cheap vodka. It had been a lousy day. He'd gotten a speeding ticket, which meant his insurance was going to go up again. His secretary had quit. Just like that, after four years. She'd given him exactly two days' notice. And to top it all off, when he'd opened the glove compartment to get the registration papers for the car, he'd found Julie's tennis bracelet. He had no idea why it was there. A present from him. Given to her on their first anniversary. She'd cried when she'd opened the box. They'd made love on the living room carpet.

But the discovery hadn't just stirred memories. It had also brought home the fact that Julie might be gone for good. That the police department and Dylan could very well come up empty. While he waited for the motorcycle cop to finish writing his ticket, Sebastian had been forced to acknowledge that possibility for the first time. The revelation hit him hard. She couldn't be gone. Not forever. Not like this. Not when she was so important to him.

He took another drink and his gaze moved to the woman's rear end, which was sticking out prominently as she leaned over the table. Something stirred in him. A dark hunger. He slapped a buck tip on the table and headed toward the blonde. At least he wouldn't be alone.

LILY FINALLY got out of bed at three-thirty. She'd slept, if you could call it that, for a couple of hours, and tried valiantly to go back to sleep, but it was no use. She might as well get something done instead of lying in bed tormenting herself.

To say she was confused was an understatement. Even the pages and pages she'd written in her diary hadn't made things clearer. Cole was an enigma, and her feelings about him were even more of a mystery.

She slipped a pair of shorts underneath her sleep shirt and headed for the kitchen. Although she couldn't precook breakfast, she could do a lot about lunch and dinner. A meat loaf, a lasagna, both could be easily reheated when needed. The cooking would keep her occupied, which would be a very good thing.

The house was dark but she found her way to the kitchen, nearly blinding herself when she turned on the lights. After a brief adjustment, she got to work. First was coffee. Then she assembled the ingredients for both dishes. That pretty much took all the counter space. She measured everything, diced onions and garlic, shredded cheese, put on a big pot of water to boil for the pasta. All the while, she thought about Cole. Big surprise.

Damn, but he could kiss. He'd about knocked her socks off. Even scarier, she'd been inches away from ripping his clothes off and throwing him to the floor.

Excellent detective work all the way around, eh? Sterling. The first thing she'd learned in the academy was not to make it personal. To distance herself from the situation. Getting involved in any way was a danger to both the agent and the civilians. So what had she done the moment she'd arrived? She'd let her curiosity sway her into a shaky course of action. She'd let her hormones lead her directly into temptation.

The water hit a rolling boil, and she put the lasagna

noodles in to cook, then set the timer. After washing her hands, she got to work seasoning the ground beef, which was messy work indeed, since she believed in using the tools God gave her and digging in with both hands.

She was pretty sure her attraction to Cole wasn't about his looks. Not that they hurt or anything, but she'd been around plenty of gorgeous guys, and never once had she wanted to jump their bones within the first fifteen minutes. She hadn't even wanted to do that with Jason.

God, Jason. One thing about fixating on Cole—it made her forget all about that SOB. She stopped kneading. Was that it? Was Cole a distraction? At home she'd been so miserable, so moody and frustrated with herself, but being here gave her a whole new focus. The job, evidently, wasn't enough. She'd needed it to be personal.

Damn, damn, damn. Talk about selfish. Her friend was dying and had asked her to do one thing. Find her grandson and bring him back home. But no. That would be too straightforward for a manipulative creature like herself. She had to pretend she wanted to have his child. She'd completely convinced herself that she had to understand him in order to get him to reconcile with Eve. The whole house of cards could tumble down with one logical breath.

She attacked the meat again, and it occurred to her that she needed something physical to do. Meat loaf didn't cut it. She needed to run or lift weights or ride. Yeah, ride. After breakfast, she'd borrow a horse. Get rid of some of this energy.

The noodles needed stirring, but first she had to wash the gunk off her hands. As she scrubbed, her thoughts went back to that first meeting. She tried to picture what would have happened if she'd simply told Cole the truth. He'd have shown her the door. She felt sure about that, and not just because she needed to rationalize her behavior.

So if her very first instincts had been on the money, where had she gone wrong? When had the situation gotten personal?

The moment he'd touched her—when she'd looked into those dark, angry eyes. Some internal switch had gone from off to on, and that's all they wrote. Biology in action.

She'd seen some documentaries on the Discovery Channel about human sexuality, and one show in particular had been about this very thing. After years of research and study, it was a mystery why one person enticed and another repulsed.

She didn't have a clue what made her want Cole. But want him, she did. Not that she was going to do anything about it. But she had to admit the truth to herself—when he kissed her, he curled her toes.

The sky was getting lighter. It was just past 5:00 a.m. The noodles had a few more minutes to cook, and then she could put together the lasagna. In the meantime, she separated the ground beef for the meat loaf and put it in another bowl. She'd add chili sauce and a few spices, then she could cook both dishes at the same time.

The timer went off, and the next half hour was Cole-free. Her thoughts were on the food, on the menu for the day. But once she put the casseroles in the oven, there was nothing else to distract her. All she was left with was dishes to wash and a head full of doubt.

COLE ATE his breakfast in silence, which wasn't unusual. He also kept his gaze on his plate, which was. Looking at Lily had side effects, and he wasn't well rested enough to handle them.

For the second night in a row, he'd slept terribly, reason enough right there for her to go. On the other hand, the morale of the men hadn't been this high since... Ever. They laughed and ate like each meal was their last, and one hell of a lot of work was getting done. That was good, because he needed them to pick up his slack.

Manny reached for another biscuit, his third, if Cole had counted correctly. "Lily, what are we having for lunch?"

"Meat loaf."

A collective ecstatic groan was heard around the table.

J.T. swallowed his mouthful and asked, "Do you make it sweet? Or spicy? My mom used to make it with ketchup, and man, it was the best. We'd have it hot at night and make sandwiches the next day."

"My mother used Worcestershire sauce." John cleared his throat as he always did when he talked about his mother. "She was a fine cook. She always made fresh mashed potatoes with meat loaf."

Cole chanced a look at Lily. She sat between Chigger and Spence. She'd finished eating, and it was clear she was enjoying the conversation. When she glanced his way, he went back to staring at the remains of his eggs, ham and hash browns.

"Spence, what about you?"

"My mother wasn't much of a cook," he said, his voice so soft you had to strain to hear him. That was

Spence. "But we had a lady who worked for us, her name was Rowena, and she was one hell of a cook."

"What'd she make?" Manny asked, leaning forward.

"Sweet potato pie. Corn bread that melted in your mouth. Macaroni and cheese. Oh, yeah. That macaroni was something else."

Cole, with his downcast eyes, listened interestedly as the men waxed on about their favorite foods. If he'd watched them, he would have missed the reverential tone, the way food was so connected to people they loved. He wouldn't short them a cook again. This was a good lesson.

But he also realized good food was only a part of the reason the men had grown nostalgic. Lily, with that way of hers, made it easy to talk. To confess. Even with that smart-ass mouth of hers, she was still the kind of person strangers would confide in.

He'd told her more than he should have. Damned if he hadn't thought about telling her everything.

"Cole?"

He looked up, and all eyes were on him. Lily must have been calling him for a while, but he'd been too lost in thought.

"What about you? How did your mother cook meat loaf?"

"She didn't." He pushed his plate away and grabbed his hat from the back of his chair as he stood. "Manny, where'd you say those fences needed fixing?"

Manny looked surprised. Tough. It was Cole's ranch, and if he wanted to fix fences, he'd damn well fix fences.

"Out by pasture two."

Cole nodded, then headed out toward the barn. He'd had enough of talking about mothers and meat loaf.

THE HORSE'S NAME was Charley, and Manny had told her he was responsive. Manny had been right. Lily barely had to touch him to get him to turn or stop. He was a beauty, too, brown with a white nose. Charley wanted to run, she could feel it in the quiver of his body, but he maintained his pace. Once she got farther out into the pasturelands, she'd give him his head.

She'd also borrowed a hat and a canteen, and was going to take full advantage of the animal, the day and the hours ahead.

It had cooled down into the nineties. This time of year in Texas, you couldn't expect much lower. She didn't care. The heat felt healing to her, as if something inside had been cold for a long time and was just now thawing out.

She rode past the cattle. Most of them were standing and chewing in the shade of the oak trees, some were lying down, some watching her ride. They were big Black Angus, prized for their beef. They made her think of home. Of her dad. He took such pride in his herd.

At the end of the first pasture, the cattle thinned out, and the countryside became more wooded. The shade made the grass greener, and she suspected there had to be springwater nearby.

She found the fence long before she found Cole. And she heard him cussing long before she saw him. When she did, she reigned in Charley and took a moment, giving homage where it was due.

He had his shirt off. That was just for starters. He was wrestling with a big fence stake, trying to beat it into submission with a huge mallet. His gloved hands made his chest look even more naked, if that was possible. Normally, Lily wasn't a big fan of sweat, but Cole's glistening body made her reconsider. The tension came back to her insides, in the hollow place she became aware of whenever she got close to him.

He swung the mallet again, and she drooled over his muscles. His biceps alone were worthy of a sonnet. If only she had a camera.

His curse jarred her, not because of the word, but because she realized she was staring with her mouth open. Literally. It was kind of embarrassing. Urging Charley forward, she called out a hello so she wouldn't scare Cole. There were no first-aid stations here, and that mallet could do some serious damage.

He jerked around to face her. There was no immediate look of welcome. Instead, he scowled. Somehow it wasn't quite fair that the frown made him more handsome. Hell, he'd be gorgeous no matter what he did.

"What are you doing here?"

"Taking a survey."

"I mean it, Lily. What the hell are you doing? Don't you have work to do at the house?"

She waited until she got a few feet from him, then dismounted. After a quick stretch, she smiled at the shirtless cowboy. "I've already done my chores, boss. Lunch is fixed and ready. Dinner is prepared, except for the salad."

"That still doesn't explain why—"

"I wanted to have a ride, okay? I needed some air."

"You'll get all you need when you ride back."

"Thanks for your concern. But before I leave, I'm going to help you with the fence."

"No, you're not."

She sighed. "Oh, Cole. You're so predictable."

He bristled. "What does that mean?"

"I knew you were going to argue with me. But you forget, I grew up on a ranch. I've fixed fences. I'm not a delicate flower that can't get her hands dirty."

"I don't care. I don't want your help."

"Sure you do."

"Didn't we make a big enough mistake last night?"

She pulled a pair of Manny's gloves out of the saddlebag and put them on. "Here's what I'd like to do. Work now, and argue later."

"I—"

She held up her hand. "I understand your concerns. But for now, let's not think of me as a woman and you as a man, okay?"

"It doesn't bother you in the least that I don't want you here?"

"Nope. So, what's this?" She tapped the rail. "Does it just have to be reseated?"

He gave her a world-class glower, then grudgingly nodded down the way a piece. "We've got about six down, and the wire needs to be replaced."

"Well, isn't that lucky? I happen to be great at replacing wire." She walked over to his horse, a beautiful stallion, and got the wire and tools from the saddle. "Now you be careful with that mallet."

She walked away, knowing he was staring at her, feeling his gaze on her butt. With turnabout being fair play, she had no right to complain, but man, was she self-conscious.

Clearly they couldn't even be in the same county without getting all worked up over each other. Maybe—and this was just an idea, nothing written in stone—maybe they should just get on with it. Do the deed. Begin the beguine. Maybe all this tension between them was just so much pent-up energy that needed to be released, and once it was, they could be around each other comfortably.

She nearly stumbled over some tangled wire and examined the situation, seeing where it would be best to start. But as soon as she began the actual work, she brought back her idea for consideration.

A little bedroom gymnastics might just be what the doctor ordered. Let them both get it out of their systems. Afterward, they'd talk without all this nonsense. All this awareness. Right?

Oh, who was she kidding? He'd have to be the worst lay in Texas for her to stop thinking about him that way. And there was no possibility of that being the case.

Once she got him in bed, she had the feeling it would take the national guard to let him go. The only solution? She didn't dare even think about heading in that direction.

She turned toward where Cole was working, but she couldn't see him. Not in the flesh. But he was there, in stunning detail in her mind's eye.

Work. Just *work*. Hard physical labor. It was her only hope.

CHAPTER ELEVEN

COLE SWUNG the mallet again and felt the vibrations up his arms and into his chest. Damn her. What was she trying to do? Did she want to force him into a corner? Or did she just want to drive him crazy?

Once more, he lifted the sledgehammer above his head, but then he looked at the rail. It was buried halfway to Sunday. He hadn't paid attention, and now he had to dig the damn thing up and start all over.

He cursed for as long as he could come up with fresh words. It was her fault. Everything was her fault. Especially the crazy thoughts that had plagued him all morning.

Putting the mallet down, he grabbed his shirt and wiped his face with it. Even in the shade it was damn hot. She probably forgot to bring water with her. Great. So she'd pass out from heatstroke, and then what was he supposed to do? Tie her to Charley and hope she'd live until the horse got back to the ranch? Like hell.

The thought of water made him aware of his own thirst, and he took care of that with one of his two canteens. He was used to working in the hot sun and he'd come prepared.

Damn woman.

What he needed to do was go find her and talk to her. Give her the speech he'd been rehearsing since last night. She'd argue with him, but in the end, she'd see he was right. This wasn't the place for her. The men would survive on their own food for a few more days. He'd go back to square one, and this time, he'd be much better prepared to find the kind of woman he was looking for.

She wouldn't be beautiful, that's for sure. She wouldn't be mouthy. She wouldn't crawl under his skin like someone he could mention.

When he thought about it, it was probably good that Lily had come to stay. He would never have been able to get so specific about what he wanted until he'd seen what he didn't want.

He took one more swig of water, letting his gaze follow the broken wire fence. It wasn't getting any cooler, so he'd better go get her. The rail would wait.

He put his supplies back on his saddle, donned his shirt, although it was too hot to button it, and hoisted himself on Phantom. The Arabian stallion had been with him for three years, and they'd grown to know each other well in that time. Good old reliable Phantom. No surprises with him.

He set out at a cautious pace, wary of loose wire. Cole relaxed, or tried to. It didn't seem possible with Lily in the same vicinity.

By the time he saw her, he'd rehearsed his speech half a dozen more times. She was on the fourth rail, and as he rode by each of the previous three, he had to admit she'd done a passable job fixing them. At least she hadn't lied about working on a ranch.

She looked up at him as he approached. Her hat shaded her eyes, but her mouth was lit by the sun. He wished he didn't know the taste of her. The feel of those lips.

Forcing his gaze down, he saw how hot she was. Sweat stained her white T-shirt under her arms and down her back. Her bra strap stood out in stark relief. The way her jeans hugged her hips made him too aware of what effect she had on him.

"You done already?"

He shook his head and reached for his second canteen. "Brought you water."

"Thanks." She walked over to him. "It's thirsty work."

"No doctors out here. Man gets heatstroke, he's pretty much done for."

"Well, it was very considerate of you." She unscrewed the cap and tilted her head back to drink. His gaze went to her neck, the smooth pale skin, the hollow at the base. He shifted in his saddle.

She finished her drink, then handed him the canteen. "I'm almost finished here," she said. "Another hour or so ought to be enough."

"Not today. Not with this heat. We'll finish another time."

"I don't mind."

"I do."

She shrugged. "You're the boss."

Damn straight.

"God, I wish you had a swimming pool," she said as she headed over to get her tools.

His gaze moved to the copse of trees dead south. An idea took hold in his head with a pit bull's teeth. He didn't even dismount and help her with the wire. Instead, he became uncomfortably aware of his own clothes sticking to his body. The sweat that made an itchy path down his back.

"Come on," he said. "There's something I want to show you."

She didn't hurry. Although he was anxious, he couldn't help but notice the care she took with the supplies. He always said you could tell a lot about a man from the way he kept his equipment.

Finally, she handed him those things she'd borrowed, then put her boot in the stirrup and swung her other leg over the saddle.

Before her butt even touched the seat, he'd urged Phantom forward. Lily would follow. He'd give her his speech there, by the spring. After they'd both cooled off a bit. If she hadn't been with him, he'd have taken off every stitch and gone swimming. Even when it was hot like this, the natural spring water kept cool.

Oh, great. Now he was picturing her in the buff. Skinny-dipping and laughing, her breasts buoyed by the water, her nipples hard with the cold. Of course, his body would react too, only in the opposite manner. Another great joke by a fickle universe.

"Cole?"

He turned his head. "Yeah."

"Where are we going?"

"You'll see."

"Just tell me one thing. Is this a good surprise?"

He nodded.

"You know what?"

"Huh?"

"You're one strange son of a bitch."

He smiled. Yeah, he did know that. But it worked, so he didn't give a damn. He had his kingdom. This parcel of land in Texas that no one could touch. He had his stock and his breeding program. If he was forced to tell the truth, he'd have to admit he wasn't a born rancher, but that was okay. He liked managing the ranch, coming up with new techniques and innovative approaches to raising cattle. Besides, he hired men who loved the work. All in all, he was proud of his accomplishments, even though there was one thing that would make the whole picture perfect.

Phantom must have felt his impatience because his pace quickened as they reached the heaviest concentration of trees. Or maybe he just smelled the water, and his thirst was getting to him. The horse led them through oaks so old they must have seen the world get born. The pointed leaves shimmered in the light breeze, and for the first time since leaving the house, Cole felt some relief from the heat.

Soon, very soon, he'd splash that cold water all over himself. He didn't care if his clothes got soaked.

He'd rather like it if hers did.

Phantom stepped over the carcass of a tree that had been felled by lightning. Right after that, he curved to the left, and a few moments later he brought them to the spring.

It wasn't big. Not like Elm Creek or anything. But it was a good half mile across, and the water was fresh and clean. He could smell it from here, and so did the horses.

"Oh, my God! This is gorgeous!"

"Yeah."

Lily dismounted and the first thing she did was remove Charley's saddle and bridle. "Go on, boy. Get yourself some water."

The kindness surprised Cole. Most of the women he'd known wouldn't have thought of an animal before their own pleasure. He shook his head as he did the same for Phantom.

"What is this?"

"A spring."

"I know that. I mean, this place?" She looked around in pure wonder, appreciating the natural beauty that had always calmed him. This was where he came to be alone. To think. The only reason she was here was that she was going back to San Antonio soon. No one came with Cole out here. Sure, the men knew about it and used it, but they also knew never to bother him here.

Her gaze moved from the blue-green water to the border of thick plants and rocks that made up the shore, then to him.

"This area is called the Callahan Divide, the boundary between the Brazos River and the Colorado Basin. Before we white men came and ruined it all, this was home to thousands of buffalo on their way to the high plains. In fact, the first business out here was selling the bones."

"For what?"

"They were used to refine sugar."

"Excuse me?"

He nodded. "I don't think they use buffalo bones anymore."

"So is this water just for drinking?" she asked, turning back to the spring. Even though he could only see her profile, the look of longing was clear.

"No, we use it for swimming. But we didn't bring any suits."

"Suits? We don't need no stinkin' bathing suits."

"Pardon?"

Her grin lit up her face. "Bastardized line from *Treasure of the Sierra Madre.*"

"I know that. I was referring to the content of your statement."

"Oh. Right. Well, I don't know about you, but I'm wearing underwear. And frankly, my underwear reveals a lot less than my bathing suit."

He could feel his cheeks heat as image after image flashed through his brain like a peep show. Sure, she could get away with underwear. He, on the other hand, wore boxers, and in his current state, there would be no mistaking what was on his mind.

"I don't think so."

"Tell you what," she said, her fingers undoing her belt buckle. "You keep your pants on. I'm going swimming."

"Lily…it's not a good idea."

"Why not?"

"Were you there last night? Or was that just me?"

"Oh, yeah." She leaned against a tree and pulled her boots off, then her socks. "That's easily fixed. Turn around."

"What?"

"Obviously, you have no self-control, so turn around. Don't watch me." As she spoke the sound of her zipper echoed to Kansas and back.

"Very amusing."

"Look, big guy. I'm really hot and sweaty, and I don't have to be. You do what you want."

"But I need to talk to you."

"Great. See you in the water."

Just as he was going to tell her to wait, she pulled her pants straight down and stepped out of them. Her legs. Oh, Lord. Her long, lean legs seemed to go on forever. As his gaze traveled up her pale, perfectly muscled thighs, his temperature rose dangerously, and when he got a load of her pale-pink satin panties, he hurt himself trying not to drool. Of course, his dilemma worsened. It would sure feel better taking his pants off. There was only so much room there. But the tent factor would make a hooker blush. Maybe he should turn around. But he couldn't. Not when she was lifting her T-shirt off.

The material rose slowly. The panties were cut high on the leg and low on her stomach. Her belly button went in, not out, and her torso was what Manny would call "ripped." Slight indents on the sides, with a soft feminine curve up the middle.

He'd been so engrossed with her stomach that he hadn't noticed her T-shirt was gone. But once he saw her bra, it was pretty much all he could think of. It matched her panties. One of his little quirks was that he was a sucker for just that. Women in matching underwear. Of course, if she'd had a garter belt, nylons and high heels, he'd probably embarrass himself right here and now. As it was, the aching in his jeans wasn't getting any better.

Her laughter made him look up from the soft mounds held by the satin material, the outline of her ripe nipples clear and irresistible. But he forced his gaze to her face, and her great big old grin.

"You are so busted."

"Huh?"

"Let's see…. Your mouth has been hanging open since my pants went down. And, uh, Cole Junior there is doing his level best to break out of prison."

He whirled around, giving her his back to contemplate. He *had* been busted, and it was his own damn fault. His cheeks filled with fire, and he cursed his libido, but even this didn't ease the strain of "Cole Junior."

Her laughter bounced off the trees as she headed toward the spring. Even though he shouldn't, he dared a look.

Big mistake. Huge error.

Her panties were thongs.

He groaned as he watched her buttocks. He could pound nails with junior, and that was no exaggeration. If he didn't cool off soon, he might permanently damage himself. Only… "The hell with it," he said, and threw his hat down and wrestled his boots off. His shirt and socks were next, and then his belt buckle.

Lily was already immersed in the water by the time he reached the edge of the spring. He could see her shadow as she swam like a little mermaid. Now was his chance. He undid his pants with care, then slipped them off. His groan was a mixture of relief and pain as he freed himself from the constraint. The moment he kicked his jeans to the side, Lily came up for air. And looked right at him. Her gaze moved down his chest, and he put his hands in front of his crotch.

She laughed out loud. Really howled.

He couldn't get any more embarrassed, so he took his hands away, revealing the Empire State Building in his shorts. Wading purposefully into the water, he didn't stop until he was a foot under.

LILY WENT UNDER, too, just to check that Cole wasn't committing suicide by drowning. She could see him clearly in the water, with his back to her. He moved his arms and legs to keep from bobbing to the surface, but not for long. Soon, he went up, and so did she.

When her head popped to the surface, she pushed her hair back with her hands, her grin absolutely uncontrollable. He was just too adorable for words. So embarrassed. She'd like to embarrass him quite frequently. His cheeks looked so cute when they were pink.

He scowled at her, but she knew his bark was worse than his bite. Such a *guy*. Anger was always first. But the good ones went through the anger until they got to the other side. Cole would find the humor in the situation. Maybe not today. Maybe not this year. But he would.

"You can stop gloating," he said with a growl that matched his expression.

"Not yet. I'm having too much fun."

"So you're a sadist, is that what you're telling me? You like making people uncomfortable, then laughing at them?"

"Not people. You."

His brows went up, and in his surprise his frown disappeared. "Why me?"

"Because you're such an easy target."

"I am not."

"Oh, please. You are so. You blush like a virgin in a bordello."

"You do know that I could drown you out here and you wouldn't be found for a long, long time."

"Right. You brute. You can't even stand the thought that I might get thirsty."

"Can't we just swim quietly?"

"Sure." She dove under again and swam to where he was treading water. Before she could stop herself, she'd yanked the back of his shorts down, taking a moment to appreciate the white butt she'd uncovered.

Then she swam away as he turned on her. She came up at the other end of the spring.

"That was infantile."

She laughed. "I know."

"You're too old for that nonsense."

"Like hell I am. In fact, it's my goal in life to be an eccentric old woman. Pulling down your underwear fits right into my long-range goals."

"I've got some short-term goals that seem pretty doable." He moved closer to her, his body slicing through the water like a seal.

She liked him wet. And truth be told, she liked him hard. She'd been unbelievably flattered at his display of lust, and secretly happy that she had no such obvious meter. She wondered if he knew that she wanted him just as much. That her insides had tightened, and that she had an awful itch that only he could scratch.

She was utterly, completely, wantonly turned on. Her fingers ached to touch him everywhere. Her body felt hollow and hungry, incomplete.

He was getting closer now. She didn't try to escape his revenge. She wasn't going to make love to him, but she sure as hell wouldn't mind some kissing. Maybe even a little touching.

"What is that look about?" he demanded.

"What look?"

He shook his head as he swam right up to her, his body inches from her own. "The one on your face. You look like you're planning something else. Something evil."

"Wicked, maybe. Evil, no."

"How wicked?"

Her smile curved up slowly as she thought of all

the possibilities. In the water, on the bank. Wet. Dry. A plethora of libidinous choices awaited them if only they would get a bit daring. If only he would. She was ready. More than ready.

Cole cleared his throat. ''I brought us here to cool us down.''

''It didn't work.''

He didn't answer her for a long time. His gaze roamed her face, searching for something, but she wasn't sure what. Permission? It was granted, couldn't he see?

Seconds ticked by and he did nothing. Made no move. She couldn't understand what he was waiting for. But she was patient. Honestly, she could wait. It wasn't as if she'd die or anything if he didn't touch her soon.

His hand brushed hers. She didn't even think it was intentional. But it was all the encouragement she needed. She swam to his chest, wrapped her arms around his neck and kissed him until she nearly drowned in pleasure.

CHAPTER TWELVE

COLE HAD to breathe. Her mouth and his were locked so tight he didn't swallow any water, but if they kept this up, they'd both drown. He kicked until their heads were above the water line, then broke away from her. "Come," he whispered. Then, the taste of her still making him crazy with want, he pulled her toward the shore. Testing the depth about three feet from land, he touched the rocky bottom, found a foothold, then pulled her into his arms and kissed her again.

She tasted like cinnamon and artesian water, and he couldn't get enough of her. It was insane, he was insane as he thrust his tongue into the warmth of her mouth, mimicking the act he desperately wanted to do. When her legs wrapped around his waist, he groaned with frustration. But he couldn't do anything in the water.

He headed toward dry land, his hands holding her virtually naked bottom. She had her arms wrapped tightly around his neck and didn't let go until he stopped at a grassy slope by an ancient oak.

Releasing her wasn't easy. He wanted her body next to his. If it were up to him, he would have simply braced her against the tree and taken her right there. His concern for her back overrode his lust, though, and so he shifted until she stood in his arms.

"We don't have towels," she whispered, her gaze fixed on his.

He shook his head. "We don't have a blanket."

She ran her hand down his chest. "Guess we'll have to let the sun dry us, huh?"

He closed his eyes as her finger circled his nipple. "Uh-huh."

"Think we should hang our clothes up in this tree?"

"Uh-huh," he repeated, not caring in the least what they did with their clothes as long as they were off. He was hard again, but this time he knew he wouldn't leave in frustration. He'd be inside her soon. The thought was so compelling he rushed to strip right there, but the moment his fingers had slipped inside the band of his shorts, she stepped back. The problem was, she hadn't stepped away so she could undress. The expression on her face told him that.

"What's wrong?"

She sighed. "I swore I wasn't going to do this."

"Are you kidding me?"

She shook her head. "No. I wish I was. I wish I could just throw you to the ground and say the hell with the consequences, but I can't."

"Is this about birth control?"

"No. I'm on the pill. This is about me. About what I'm here for."

He closed his eyes again, trying like hell to defuse the near crisis situation in his heated body.

"I'm sorry," she said. "It's all my fault. I was an incredible tease, and I should never have done that. I know better."

When he opened his eyes, she had walked several feet away. She'd folded her arms across her chest, and he could see she felt too naked in front of him. "Care to explain?"

Lily struggled to put her feelings into words, but it was difficult. She hardly understood them herself. She wanted him. Oh my, yes. She wanted him like crazy. But the warning bell had gone off. Some part of her had made her pull away.

The fact was, she wasn't that experienced. Jason was only the second man she'd been with. The first had been Michael Kelper, her high school sweetheart, the boy she'd loved with all her heart and soul. They'd done it the night they'd graduated, and it had been horrible. Neither of them had known what they were doing, and she'd come away thinking, "Is that it? Is that what all the fuss is about?" It wasn't until Jason that she understood there was something great about sex. But she'd put off sex with him until she'd fallen for his charm. For his honeyed words. Until she'd been in love.

"Lily? I thought—"

"Cole, I don't want you to be the rebound guy."

"What are you talking about?"

"Jason. I told you about him."

"The married guy?"

"Yeah. The thing is, I didn't tell you this all happened just a few months ago. I promised myself I wouldn't get involved with anyone for at least a year. Only, I didn't count on meeting you."

"I thought we were talking about sex. Not romance."

She sucked in a sharp breath. "Wow. Yeah. That is what we were talking about. Completely. And there's nothing wrong with that. We're both adults, and it's really obvious we're attracted to each other...."

"But?"

She looked at him with regret. Soft longing. "I'll never want to just have sex. I only want to make love. And I can't have that with you."

A dozen arguments came to mind, but he kept his mouth shut. She'd said no. That was the end of that. But he couldn't keep looking at her in her transparent underwear, her body slick and wet.

He walked away, out of the shade. Out of her reach. Not trusting himself to speak. Then he sat himself down and closed his eyes. He'd dry off soon enough, and then he'd get dressed and head on back to the ranch.

"Cole?"

She was close, just a foot away. "Yeah?"

"You had something to tell me, didn't you?"

Now she was next to him on the grass. He didn't dare look at her. Not if he wanted to get the speech right. He ran it through his head quickly. She wasn't the right woman. It was best if she left. As if she needed more proof than her own words. Of course, he'd pay her for her services....

"Cole?"

He opened his eyes. Turned to look at her. She was very close, sitting down, hugging her knees. So beautiful it made him wish he was someone else. Someone who could fall in love. But he wasn't. And it was high time he told her to go. He took a deep breath and let it out slowly. But instead of beginning the well-rehearsed speech, he felt a stillness inside his chest, something he couldn't remember feeling before. The way she looked at him, with a compassion that was completely new territory, made him think crazy thoughts. Like talking to her. Like telling her everything.

She just waited. If she'd said anything, he probably would have recited his canned speech. But she didn't.

"Five years ago, I caught my father in bed with my fiancée."

The words hung in the air. He could hardly believe he'd said them. Not to her. Not to anyone. What had happened between him and Carrie was his own private hell.

"Oh, honey," Lily whispered.

Her tone made his chest constrict. He lay back and stared at the sky, wondering if he'd lost his mind. A few clouds billowed far to the east. Above him was nothing but blue. "We'd been together for two years. Engaged for six months. I met her at a fund-raiser for a children's charity my family supported. Everything about her was perfect. I remember thinking that exact thing the first time I laid eyes on her. She had blond hair, the kind that looks like wheat. Big blue eyes, a warm smile. She wasn't obvious, though. In fact, she made me work at getting her to go out with me. And then she held out for the ring. But that was okay. I wanted to marry her. I was in love with her."

The clouds were getting closer. Or maybe not. He couldn't trust his perceptions from this angle. It didn't matter. The sun was doing its job, drying him off. Lily wasn't hugging her knees anymore. Out of the corner of his eye, he saw she'd lain down parallel to him, but not too close.

"Then what?" Lily asked, her voice filled with that same kindness.

"Then we started planning the wedding. It was going to be big, and for her it became a full-time job. She and my grandmother worked together. I kept out of it.'' He touched the waistband of his shorts. Still damp, but nothing major. It was time to turn over.

After he was settled again, with his chin on his folded arms, he wondered if he should go on. He'd told her more, much more than he'd intended. But there was something about Lily that made it okay. Actually, talking to her made him feel better.

''Where was it supposed to be held?''

''At my grandmother's. No expense was spared. My mother was gone—she was killed in a car accident—and my father, he wasn't around very much. At least, so I thought. Then, about two months before the wedding, Carrie told me she was pregnant.''

''Oh, God.''

''Yeah. At first, I didn't think too much about it. We were going to be married anyway. I didn't care. But then I went with her when she had her sonogram. I saw the baby's heart beat. And man, I'd never wanted anything so badly in all my life. I went nuts. I started buying him toys and planning his future. I couldn't believe my luck, to have found this perfect woman and to make a son with her. It was everything I ever wanted.''

''Cole—''

He couldn't stop now. The whole thing had to come out. To be laid bare on the parched earth. ''Three weeks before the wedding, I came home early from a business trip to Houston. I was a management consultant then. The man I was going to see had gotten sick. We rescheduled the meeting, and I caught the first plane out of there. I didn't bother to call

Carrie, but I did get her flowers. Pink roses, two dozen. Her favorite.

"I got home and I saw the light on in the bedroom. So I hid the flowers behind my back and snuck over to the door. I heard something, but I couldn't tell you exactly what. Just that it made my blood run cold. I opened the door, and at first I didn't see who she was with. It was just some man. Some other man. But then he looked up at me. My own goddamn father. He was still—" Suddenly, he couldn't speak anymore. In fact, he didn't want much of anything except to go back to when he was numb.

"How could he do that?" Lily sat up again. "The stupid bastard. How could he do that to his own son?"

"I don't know. I never asked him."

"But what about the child?"

He laughed bitterly. "Yeah. The boy..."

Lily waited. He'd tell her in his own time. She was still trying to understand what had happened. How a father could do something so despicable to his own son. "I can't..." She didn't have a clue what to say. "Sorry" didn't cut it by half. Of course he didn't trust anyone. How could he? The level of that betrayal went all the way to the core. To the depths of the soul.

So much of his behavior made sense now. Why he wanted no attachments to a mate. Why he wanted a son of his own. What had seemed eccentric and a little nuts only moments before now had a desperate logic.

She longed to touch him. To hold him close and ease his pain. But there was no touch of hers that could heal him. He'd have to do that for himself. "What happened to the boy?"

Cole finally looked at her, and it was all she could do to stop herself from bursting into tears. His expression was so raw, so hurt.

Her brother Dylan was like Cole. For them, love is everything—unequivocal, complete and guileless. It didn't matter which facade they used as protection—Dylan with his sense of humor and his easy smile, or Cole with his granite mask—they were more vulnerable than they would ever admit.

She said a silent prayer of thanks that she'd stopped Cole and herself from going too far. Despite what he'd said, this wasn't just about sex. If it had been, he wouldn't have told her his story. He wouldn't have had to turn away from her.

"I'll tell you something. Despite everything, I still wanted that boy. Crazy, huh?"

"No, not really. I suppose you'd already sort of fallen in love with him."

Cole nodded, then put his chin on his arm again. "I knew it was my father's fault. He was such a manipulative bastard, Carrie didn't stand a chance. I knew she had to be feeling guilty as hell. But I couldn't stay there, not while I was so angry. I thought I might kill him."

He grew quiet then, and she could almost imagine what he was thinking about. She understood betrayal. Being lied to. Being stupid and naive. What she couldn't imagine was that betrayal coming from someone in her own family.

"I went to California for a couple of weeks. I had a friend in Laguna Beach who lent me his house. I did a lot of thinking. A hell of a lot of walking. And the more I thought about it, the more I was sure I could never get past it. Not as far as my father was concerned. I never wanted to see him again. And I wasn't sure I wanted to see Carrie, either.

"My grandmother told me to buck up. To accept the situation and grow from it. To come back and act as if nothing had happened. She said it was my duty as a Bishop to carry on. To raise the child on my own and never speak of the unpleasantness again. I'd never heard her so angry as when I told her no."

The sun finally got to Lily, and she turned over. She was terribly thirsty, but there was no way in hell she was going to move away from him to get water.

"As it turned out, it wasn't over. Not by a long shot. I got a letter from my grandmother about four days before I was supposed to head back. Carrie had lost the baby. She'd miscarried. And she and my father had gotten married in Las Vegas."

Lily had no more words. Everything seemed inadequate. Foolish.

"Eve—that's my grandmother—didn't care for that last bit, and from the last letter I opened from her, the marriage had been annulled. I never spoke to my father again."

"What about you and the others? Carrie. Your grandmother?"

He shook his head. "I did end up opening the last letter Carrie sent me. Turns out the story I'd been given wasn't exactly the truth. There was no miscarriage. Eve paid for the abortion, and she paid for Carrie to disappear. I've never spoken to my grandmother again, either."

"But surely after all this time... She's your only family."

"I have no family."

"But—"

Cole stood, dusted his stomach and knees, even though there was nothing on them. "I think we're dry enough to go back now."

She nodded, and while she should have been thinking of how to convince Cole that seeing Eve was the right thing, despite the mistakes his grandmother made, she couldn't get past her own reaction to his pain. She ached for him, right down to her bones.

She'd grown up so privileged. Her family cared for her with love and tenderness, with enough discipline thrown in for her to have a good future. She'd always been able to turn to her father, her mother. Dylan and Ashley were there for her whenever she needed them.

Oh, she'd made mistakes. Transferring to the FBI offices in Dallas to follow Jason was a big one. Heck, just being with Jason at all had been a mistake. Growing up, she'd committed a hundred minor infractions, and all of them had been dealt with swiftly and fairly. She understood the concept of consequences, and it had made all the difference. She'd always known, deep in her heart, that everything would be all right. It was the fundamental truth about her life.

How could someone recover from a nightmare like Cole's? When the betrayal had come from the people who were supposed to love and protect him? No wonder there was such a wall around his heart. The question was, could the wall be toppled? Was seeing Eve—forgiving her—the one ingredient that might just save him?

She forced herself from her reverie and saw that Cole was already dressed. He was saddling Charley for her, while his own mount stood nearby. She got up and slipped on her socks, her jeans, her T-shirt. Then she found a rock to sit on while she put on her boots. The whole time, she watched Cole. Admired the way he moved, the inherent grace of the man.

She wanted to fix him. To make the ugliness disappear. But she also knew that his plan, while it had a certain logic, would ultimately be the worst thing for him.

Cole needed to work through his anger. He needed to see that his father was sick, and that Cole himself had done nothing wrong. He hadn't deserved any part of that tragedy.

Not that she was the one to help him, despite her wish to. He needed someone trained in this sort of thing. She'd had a psychology class or two, but this was out of her league. The only thing she could offer him was her friendship. And the possibility of helping him reconcile things with Eve.

"What's this?"

She turned to Cole. In his hand, he held the canteen she'd brought from the ranch this morning. "Oh. It's water."

"I can see that. Why didn't you tell me you had your own?"

"Because I didn't want to spoil your gesture. It was lovely of you to think about me like that."

"Lovely. Right."

She pushed herself off the rock and stamped her left boot to get the right fit. "Yes. Lovely. Kind. Considerate."

"Bull." He put the canteen back on her saddle. "It wasn't even about you. I just didn't want to have to carry you back to the ranch."

She approached him as gingerly as if he'd been a

wild stallion. He took a couple of steps back, but then he waited. His gaze wary, his back stiff and straight, he let her touch his arm. "Listen up, cowboy. I know you're not the SOB you pretend to be. Don't worry. I won't tell anyone. But you don't have to get all prickly with me. I understand."

His grateful smile made her feel like a million bucks.

"Lily?"

"Yes, Cole?"

"No offense, but, lady, you're full of crap."

COLE DIDN'T say much on the way back to the ranch. He was too busy wondering what in hell had gotten into him. He'd told Lily things he'd sworn he'd take to the grave. And now she knew. She knew his secrets, and with that came power. Instead of the relief he sought, he'd made himself vulnerable. What an ass. What a stupid miserable ass.

He looked over at Lily. Her gaze was on the trees, the big oaks that made this part of the country famous. That long neck of hers tried to seduce him again. Her smile was just as dangerous.

She made it too easy. No one was that good a listener. He wasn't sure how, but she'd manipulated him. And that was the issue, wasn't it?

No woman should be that close. Especially not someone as cunning as Lily. Oh, man. She made it look real. Her eyes, her voice, the way she touched him. All of it designed with one thing in mind—to trap him.

Maybe this was good, though. Maybe he needed to revise his plan. Just hire a surrogate. Forget the rest. Hire a male nanny. Plenty of kids grew up fine without a mother, as long as they had a father who was there. One who gave a damn.

He realized she was staring at him. Her brows had come down in concern, and her lips curved into a worried frown.

"What's wrong?" she asked.

"Nothing."

Silence. Then, "Okay."

Why did she back off so easily? That wasn't like her. Nosy. That's what she was. Why did she want to know so much about him? Who the hell was she?

He spurred Phantom to a quicker pace, anxious to get home. He'd figure out what to do when he was alone. Away from the smell of her, the memory of her skin.

Damn, he still couldn't believe he'd told her. That he'd laid himself bare. Then he thought about her face. How she'd looked at him. Could that kind of compassion be faked? Of course it could. But what if she wasn't—

No. No way was he going to let himself believe in her. Trust her. He'd already gone too far, and even though that couldn't be undone, he could do plenty to ensure it wouldn't come back to bite him on the butt. If he had to drive her to San Antonio himself, he would. She was gone. Out of his life. Out of his thoughts.

He passed the oak with Manny and Rita's initials carved in the bark, the boy's open declaration of his love. Cole had given him hell for damaging the tree, but Manny hadn't cared. He was crazy in love, and his dreams were as innocent as a sapling. The kid loved the ranch. More than Cole did, he often thought. He wanted to have his own place someday, just like the Circle B, and marry his girl and have a houseful of kids.

Cole hoped he got his wish. That Rita turned out to be the sweet thing Manny thought she was. Cole had to remind himself that there were fine and decent people in the world. Aside from his men, he tended to believe the rest of the human race was suspect. Untrustworthy. Yeah, the brush he painted the world with was awful big, but better to be too cautious than stupid.

There was a chance that Lily was a good woman. That she had only his best interest at heart. But it was a small chance. One he wasn't willing to take.

CHAPTER THIRTEEN

LILY HEADED back to the house from the barn, anxious for a shower and to get to her journal. The ride back had been tense, but she hadn't said a word to Cole about it.

Of course he'd pulled back. Proud as he was, it must have taken everything he had to tell her about his past. About his father. The defenses had come back up immediately, and it was no use trying to convince him that she'd never use his secrets against him.

She'd leave him be for tonight. Then, maybe tomorrow, or the day after, she'd broach the subject again. By then he'd have had time to process what had happened. If only he'd see that talking to her had opened a door that had been bolted shut. With luck, the conversation today would lead directly to a reconciliation between Cole and Eve. More than ever, Lily understood that her task was hugely important. Only it was Cole who needed her success most. It would ease Eve's heart, but it might just save Cole's life.

Manny stood by the door as she walked into the house. He smiled at her in a way that made her feel warm inside. Like she was already a friend. "How'd it go?"

She nodded. "Pretty well, although I didn't finish.

But there's only about two hours more work to be done."

"That's great. Me and Spence'll go out there to-morrow."

"Did you guys eat the meat loaf?"

His grin broadened. "Yes, ma'am. Made myself a great big old sandwich, and when I finished that, I had another. Chigger ate three."

"Wow. I'm glad it was a hit. Is there any left?"

"Some." He opened the fridge and took out a can of root beer and the covered plate of meat loaf. "Want a drink?"

"Diet, please. I'll just have a sandwich, then I need to go shower."

"So where's the boss?"

"Taking care of Phantom. I think he said he needed to go check on a bull."

Manny nodded, then crooked his head to the left. "You thinking about staying?"

"Maybe."

"For, you know…" He pointed his soda can in the general direction of her stomach.

"Maybe. But most likely not."

"But don't you think—" He looked at the door, out the window, then back at her. "Don't you think it's crazy?"

"A little."

He snorted. "I think it's a lot crazy. I mean, I want kids, too. But the whole damn reason I want them is so that Rita and I can raise them together. So they'll be our kids, you know?"

"Yeah. I do. But everyone's different, Manny. We all need different things."

"If you ask me, what he needs is a good woman."

Manny's gaze and the arch of his right brow let her know just who he was referring to.

"Nope. Sorry. Not me."

"Why not? I know it doesn't look like it, but Cole, he's a good man. He takes care of us like you wouldn't believe. I mean, we have medical and dental, you know? And every Christmas he gives us a piece of the pie, a big old bonus. He never asks too much, and he only gets angry when we've done something that deserves it. He'd be a good husband, I know it."

She couldn't help smiling at his earnestness. "You do, huh?"

He got her diet soda, popped open the top, then handed it to her. "I surely do. People just don't know Cole, that's all. That's why they talk about him. 'Cause they don't know him."

"Who talks about him?"

"Damn near everyone in town. You wouldn't believe the stories. Some say he killed a man. Did you know that?"

"I'd heard something about it. But it's not true."

"Nope. It's not. At least, I don't think so. But if he did, there was a damn good reason."

"Why don't you ask him?"

"Huh?"

"Ask him. Instead of wondering."

Manny shook his head. "Oh, no. Cole doesn't talk about himself. Not ever. He hates it if anyone brings up his family or his past."

"I still think you should ask. You're his friend. You should be able to talk about these things. Rumors don't do anyone any good."

"I know. Rita says the same thing. But I can't. It would be intruding, you know?"

"It could be more like concern. Friendship."

Manny didn't look convinced. "I'll think about it."

"You do that. I have the feeling Cole needs someone to confide in."

"It won't be me."

"Maybe not." She got a couple of slices of bread from the loaf, then scooted by Manny to get the mayo out of the fridge. "Do me a favor and try, okay? Try to be his friend. After I'm gone, I mean."

"I thought you were gonna stay?"

"It's a long shot. I'll probably leave as soon as he hires a cook."

"Oh, man. I almost forgot. I gotta tell him the agency called. Someone's coming out tomorrow."

Lily's stomach took a dip. She didn't want him to hire someone new, and she didn't want to leave. Which was incredibly dumb. For heaven's sake, they were both the walking wounded. And they both needed lots of time to heal.

Anyway, a man like Cole would have a hell of a time trusting a woman, and if there wasn't trust in a relationship, then there wasn't a relationship.

"I'll go catch up with him," Manny said. "See you at dinner. Oh, and thanks again for the meat loaf. Man, you're a *milagro* in the kitchen."

"Wow. No one's ever said I was a miracle before. Thanks."

Manny gave her his Tom Cruise grin, then walked out, slamming the back door behind him. Lily took a sip of cold soda, finished making her sandwich, and headed toward the back of the house and her bedroom, eating as she walked. She felt a bit desperate about her shower. And then there was dinner to put together. She needed to reheat the lasagna and make a salad and garlic bread. But first, her journal. There was a lot to understand, a lot to think about. And a ticking clock. Cole might just want to hire that new cook tomorrow, and then what would she do?

She'd have to talk to him in the next twenty-four hours, that's what.

COLE WATCHED HER all during dinner. She laughed and talked artfully with the others, making even shy J.T. comfortable enough to discuss his childhood, which had been no picnic. She was good. Damn good.

Chigger and Manny kept eyeing him. At first, he thought Lily had told them about his father, but then he dismissed that. It wouldn't make sense for her to do something so obvious. But they were thinking something.

The only thing that distracted him from his watchfulness was the lasagna. It was the best he'd ever had, and he was hungry as a bear. When he'd gotten back, he hadn't taken any time for lunch, grabbing an apple on his way to his office. Luckily, there was plenty, because everyone had seconds, and some had thirds.

Lily made sure their plates and glasses were full, ate her own meal, and managed to swing the conversation around to the topic of Manny's fiancée. But Cole wasn't fooled. He knew Lily didn't care about Rita. She wanted to hear Manny go on about how he loved her. How marriage was his dream, and how he wanted so many kids. And she wanted to see Cole's reaction.

He had none. What Manny did with his life was his own affair.

Finally, the food and the chatter wound down. It was Spence's night to do dishes, but nobody seemed inclined to leave him to it. Even Chigger had a second cup of coffee.

Lily brought the coffeepot over to Cole. She stood just to his left, her body close, but not touching. "More?"

He nodded.

She leaned slightly forward to pour, and that's when she brushed against his arm. He stiffened, his senses immediately heightened. Her scent filled him, not the coffee's. Everything else dimmed as his concentration focused.

She put her hand on his shoulder. Just rested it softly. She'd finished pouring the coffee. It didn't feel as though she had any intention of moving.

He gave no indication that even that small touch had caused a riot inside him. But when her fingers squeezed gently, he let his hand drop below the table. He touched the back of her thigh.

She kept standing there. Chigger told one of his horrible jokes, and the others laughed. Then J.T. brought up the Abilene Rodeo, and with all the jabbering it was a wonder anyone heard anything.

Cole tuned them out. It wasn't a choice. He couldn't hear anything but his own heartbeat. As the seconds ticked by, the reasons for telling her to leave faded. His suspicion felt foolish, paranoid. But mostly, he wanted her. Dammit, all it had taken was a touch.

DESPITE BEING bone tired, Lily couldn't sleep. She couldn't stop her feverish thoughts. She couldn't make Cole leave her be.

It wasn't all that late. Just past eleven. Dylan would be out or at his desk. No way would he be sleeping. She sat up in bed, turned on the light and got her cell phone from the dresser drawer.

He answered on the third ring. "Lily?"

"Yeah."

"Damn, I'm glad it's you. Don't you check your voice mail anymore?"

She hadn't. Not in two days. She'd been so wrapped up in—

"I have some bad news."

Her heart thudded in her chest. Oh, God. Was it their father? Ashley? Or, even more likely, was it Julie? "Tell me."

"Eve had a stroke."

The air left her lungs in a rush as she absorbed the information. "Is she—"

"She's okay. It doesn't seem to be too bad. She was at the doctor's office when it happened. Actually, in the lobby, but they got to her real fast. She has some trouble talking right now, but that could clear up all by itself. They won't know much for a couple of days."

"But she's going to live, right?"

"Yeah. Unless…"

"What?"

"Unless she has another stroke."

"God, this sucks."

"Yeah. It would be a good time to bring her long-lost grandson back to the fold. Give her a reason to fight."

"I haven't brought the subject up yet."

"What are you waiting for?"

"I was waiting for the right time. Now I don't have much choice, do I?"

"I spoke to the doctor. She's gonna need some rest for the next couple of days. He thinks she's strong and that she might end up moving a little more slowly, but that's it. So you take the time you need. It's more important that he shows up, and if you rush it—"

"Right. I'll do my best." She shifted on the bed until her feet were on the floor. "How are things with you?"

"About the same."

"Damn."

"I've been interviewing for the assistant. So far, nothing."

"You'll find the right person."

"Sebastian came by last night."

Lily wasn't bothered by the non sequitur. But she was bothered by Dylan's tone. "Is he doing any better?"

"Yeah. He is."

"And?"

"That's what's bothering me. He is doing better. He looks like he's sleeping, and he's put back some of the weight he lost."

"Why is this not a good thing?"

"Because I think he's decided Julie is gone for good."

She closed her eyes, not wanting to ask the next question. "Do you?"

He didn't answer right away. She heard him breathing. In the background, probably from his computer CD, she heard Erik Satie. "No," he said finally. "I don't. I think she's alive. I think she's in trouble."

"Then you'd best keep looking for her, little brother."

"I will."

"Keep me up-to-date about Eve, would you?"

"Of course. If you'll check your voice mail."

"I will. Good night, Dylan. Tell Dad I miss him."

"Night."

She clicked off the cell phone and put her hand in her lap. The news about Eve played havoc with her thoughts. Aside from the very real fact that Eve was a friend, and that Lily selfishly wanted her to be well, the stroke made everything here infinitely more dire.

Eve might be fine.

She might not.

Cole had to have a chance to talk to her. To make peace. Eve had to see him, to hear his voice and see how strong and capable he was. And it was all up to Lily.

She'd tell him. Tomorrow. Not in the morning, though. After he'd finished work. Chigger had told her the guys weren't going to be there for dinner. They were leaving early, going to a poker game in Buffalo Gap. She'd have Cole to herself so she could talk to him without interference.

She'd have to think long and hard about what to say. He knew she was from San Antonio. Was it so out of the question that she would know Eve? Perhaps she could mention it casually, as if she hadn't made the connection between them.

No. No lies. She'd tell him everything. And then it was up to him. She couldn't force him to see Eve. Ultimately, it was none of her business.

Who knew what had been left unsaid today by the spring? Maybe Cole had even more reason for not speaking to Eve. Something he hadn't told her. But she doubted it. In fact, her intuition made her almost frantic to put the two of them together.

Tomorrow night. Eve would be all right for one more day. She had to be.

COLE SPENT most of the next day on the phone, taking care of business he'd neglected since Lily had arrived. It was a relief to think about cattle and feed and the payroll. To wrap his mind around problems he could solve. Hell, he'd been so happy to be at work again that he'd let the men go into town a couple of hours early. Never let it be said that Cole Bishop wasn't one hell of a boss. Of course, it also didn't hurt that there was no one around to give him a raised eyebrow or a lecherous grin. They all thought he'd slept with Lily. Wouldn't they be disappointed to know the truth.

He turned off his computer at five minutes to four, but only because the woman applying for the cook's job was due. He headed toward the house, wondering if Lily would be in the kitchen.

He'd had lunch in his office, and except for breakfast, he hadn't seen her. He hadn't wanted to. It would only make his task more difficult. The plan was to hire the applicant, regardless of recommendations or suitability, and send Lily on her way. After she was gone, he'd be himself again. Things would go back to normal.

The kitchen was empty except for the intoxicating aroma of baking bread. It made him hungry all over again. With any luck, the new cook would be able to bake bread, too. And peach pie. Lily might even be willing to share her recipes. No. Not a good idea.

He went into the living room, and was pleased to find the scent of bread followed him there. After he put his hat on the console, he got his briefcase and pulled out his employee questionnaire. A sound made him look up from his paperwork, but it wasn't Lily. Disappointment hit his solar plexus with the power of a KO punch.

Dammit. Dammit all to hell. He didn't want to want her. He didn't want to be excited to see her. He didn't want to feel anything for her at all.

The doorbell saved him further torment, and just before he opened the door he was able to pull his focus away from *her*. The woman who smiled at him was in her fifties. Her dark hair was very short, almost a buzz cut, and her eyes were large behind tortoise-shell glasses.

"Mr. Bishop? I'm Virginia Holt."

He nodded, remembering his manners. "Yes. Come in, please."

She nodded, stepped inside, then followed him to the living room. After handing him an envelope, she sat on the couch, putting her large purse beside her.

He found her résumé inside the envelope, and what he read eased his mind considerably. She'd been a cook for several large ranches, including the King Ranch. She'd been at each job for at least five years. The recommendations that followed glowed. "Why did you leave your last job, Mrs. Holt?"

"My daughter got pregnant. She lives in Abilene with her husband, and I wanted to be closer to her. It's my first grandchild."

"I see."

"May I ask how many of you there are?"

"Most of the time, five or six. But at roundup—"

"I know all about roundup. I can cook for six or sixty. As long as I have control over the pantry, you never need to worry about that."

"Good." He sat down, ready to hire her on the spot. But it might worry her if he was too eager. "Do you have any specialties?"

"Like the bread I smell coming from the kitchen?"

He smiled. "Yes."

"You not only get me, Mr. Bishop, you get my sourdough starter, which some people consider worth the price of my salary. I bake bread as well as pastries. I like a varied menu using the local produce. I make sure the food I serve is nutritious, but frankly, and pardon my bragging, no one's ever noticed the nutrition part. They've just asked for seconds."

"Speaking of salary..." They discussed terms, and although her fee was a great deal more than any cook he'd had before, he'd be a fool to let her go. She was everything the ranch needed. She'd even clean up around the house, as long as he got someone in to do the heavy work.

He folded the papers and put them back in the envelope. As he looked up to make his offer, Lily appeared in the hallway. He wasn't sure how long she'd been there. My God, she was so beautiful. But she seemed terribly sad. He wanted to go to her, comfort her. Something was wrong.

"Mr. Bishop?"

He jerked his head toward Mrs. Holt. She seemed perplexed. "Yes? What?"

She cleared her throat. "I was asking about the accommodations."

"Right." He looked back at Lily. She was closer now, although not in the living room yet. She stared at him as she pushed her hair back with both hands. The movement caused her T-shirt to rise so he got the smallest glimpse of her stomach. His reaction was way out of proportion. He'd seen her nearly naked, so why was he so upset about that little flash of skin?

"Mr. Bishop?"

He'd done it again. He turned to Mrs. Holt. She smiled at him, then glanced at Lily. By the time she looked at him again, he'd decided. "I'm sorry, Mrs. Holt. You're eminently qualified for the position, but I'm not sure this would be the place for you."

She shot a look at Lily. "I see."

"I hope so. But if things change, and you're still available..."

"Of course."

She rose, and he walked her to the door. He had to consciously slow down and not shove the poor woman out. Finally, she was gone, and he hadn't embarrassed himself too badly. Lily was in the living room, looking at him with that sadness he'd noticed before.

"Why didn't you hire her?"

"She wasn't really qualified."

"But you said—"

"I don't want to talk about Mrs. Holt."

"No?"

He shook his head. "I want to—"

"What?"

"Nothing. Look, I've got more work to do, so I'd better..." He walked past her, intending to go back to his office and stay there. Already, some part of him was aware of how stupid he'd just been. He'd had the perfect cook and he'd—

Lily stopped him with a hand on his arm. All

thoughts of cooks and work fled until he was left with one word. One thought. One desire.

He turned slowly.

Her lips parted.

And he kissed her.

CHAPTER FOURTEEN

THE DRUG that was Lily flowed through his system, melting his resolve, blurring his reason, threatening his sanity. He didn't care.

He drank her in with his kisses, wallowed in her taste, her scent. As if by their own will, his hands ran down her back, underneath her T-shirt so he could feel her flesh. He groaned as he explored her back.

He felt her fingers on the back of his neck as she pressed him tighter against her lips, until he knew he must be hurting her. But her fingers, cool and long and wicked, slipped into his hair, sending chills down his body. The world could end and he wouldn't care. He wouldn't let her go.

Insanity. That's what it felt like. He was crazy, intoxicated, desperate. He rubbed her with his hips, letting her feel the way she was killing him. Then he forced himself to pull back. "What have you done to me?"

"I don't know. But you've done it back."

"I can't stand it anymore." He opened his eyes, and it surprised him that they'd been closed. Her gaze met his and he saw his own need replicated in her dilated pupils. Her cheeks were infused with a flush of red, as were her lips. Moist, slightly parted, they nearly sent him over the edge.

She stepped slightly closer and put her free hand on his chest. "Look at me," she said.

He did. He couldn't have looked anywhere else if he tried. He stood, mesmerized as her hand moved down from his chest to his waist. Past his belt. Down his fly. Until she molded her hand around his thick, constricted penis.

His groan came from deep inside, a place he'd never known. He'd wanted before, been mad for relief, but this...this was beyond endurance.

"I want you this much," she said, squeezing him gently. "But—"

He kissed her objection away. Kissed her and pressed her hand between his hard length and her stomach.

Then she stepped back, out of his arms, out of his reach. His whole body reacted with despair. They'd already stepped off the cliff. She couldn't possibly want to stop now.

But then she lifted her hand, and when he took hold of her, she led him down the hallway. The entire million steps to his bedroom.

SHE CLOSED the bedroom door and shut out the last of her misgivings. Whatever happened after, she wouldn't regret this. Her body literally ached for him. She wasn't stupid, she knew that making love to him was going to infinitely complicate their relationship, but even so, she knew she was doing the right thing.

Her intuition had been there her whole life, guiding her, warning her. If she'd only listened with Jason, she would have saved herself a mountain of heartache. Her sixth sense had never been stronger than it was right now. She *needed* to be with Cole. It didn't mean things were going to be peachy from now on. In fact, she thought the lesson might be far more harsh than she could imagine. But it was a lesson she had to learn. With this man. Now.

She turned to face him. He seemed electrified, as if there were megawatts of energy flowing just under his skin. What got to her the most was that he was waiting for her lead. She could see how much he wanted to just rip his clothes off, but his hands were by his sides. Flexing into fists, yes, but at his sides nonetheless. He wasn't going to make a move until she gave him the go-ahead.

The best way to do that seemed to be with a non-verbal approach. She kicked off her right boot.

By the time she'd taken off her left, Cole's shirt was in the corner, and he nearly keeled over in his haste to remove his own boots.

She didn't blame him. In fact, she felt the same intense need to be naked. To be next to him. No, not even that. To have him inside her. That's what the rush was about. She shivered from the inside out and squeezed her legs together, then dispensed with her T-shirt, which was followed by her jeans.

When she reached behind her back to unclasp her bra, Cole stopped her. "Wait."

She did. She put her hands down as he looked at her. His perusal was thorough. His dark eyes took in her face, then her neck. When he reached her breasts, the examination stopped.

Her nipples were so hard she thought they might poke holes in her bra. She was built more for speed than comfort, so her breasts weren't going to make the front page of any paper. But they were still firm, and dammit, they were sensitive. Right now, beneath his intense focus, she had goose bumps on her goose bumps.

His mouth opened slightly as he stepped toward her. For some reason she couldn't explain, the man still had his pants on. But she'd take care of that. Later. He was going to touch her. With his hands? His lips? Either one was fine by her as long as he did it *now*.

It was his hands. The flat of his palms, to be precise. And they rubbed the tips of her nipples in slow circles. She leaned forward to press his hands to her, but he backed away, forcing her to be still. To let him do it his way. "You bastard."

He smiled. "You haven't seen anything yet."

She moaned as she closed her eyes.

His hands disappeared. "Look at me."

She obeyed. He touched her again.

"Don't close your eyes. I want you to see everything I'm going to do to you."

"And what would that be?"

"You'll find out."

His hands kept circling, and the sensation in her breasts was like fire and ice. The circles got tighter and faster, and it was as if he were winding her up like a toy. Her insides were going berserk. She couldn't shift enough to get any relief between her legs, and she couldn't make him change the pressure on her breasts. Torture. That's what it was. Sweet, incredible torture.

His hands stilled. He reached behind her back, and in one fluid motion undid her bra. Then he moved his attention to the straps, easing them over her shoulders. He hesitated there, rubbing the bare skin where the straps had been. The only thing holding her bra up was her arms, held tight against her sides. He brought his hands down her chest, cupped her breasts, then slipped the bra off.

She had no idea where it went after that. All she could think of was the cool air, and Cole's gaze, on her naked flesh.

"You're perfect."

She grinned. "I'm already a sure thing. You don't have to woo me with flattery."

His low chuckle excited her in a totally different way. "What am I going to do with you?"

"You want that alphabetically?" He moved his hands back to her breasts, and she sighed. "I couldn't help notice—"

But he didn't care what she noticed. His lips stole her words and her breath. He rubbed his chest against her, the smattering of hair just enough to make the sensation fully arousing.

She'd seen pictures of guys built like Cole, all hard muscle, but this was her first experience with one in the flesh, so to speak. It was a little daunting, but she'd manage somehow.

He ran his hands down her back and cupped her buttocks. She still had her panties on, and that seemed to bother him. But instead of doing the sensible thing and ripping them off her, he took a somewhat different tack. He slipped his fingers underneath the leg bands, and then he pulled the material up, giving her a wedgie. But it wasn't like any wedgie she'd ever heard of. This was...

Oh, my.

He gathered the material in one hand, then eased his hand between them, doing the same maneuver with the front of her panties.

As she leaned into his kiss, he moved the material back and forth, rubbing her just enough to make all the other parts of her body jealous.

She moaned, breaking the kiss, focusing totally on her panties. Silly her. She'd always just thought of them as underwear.

Cole pulled a little tighter and rubbed a little faster. And because she was a quick study, she found herself moving, too. A little, not a lot. Putting pressure where pressure was supposed to be felt.

Her breathing escalated and her limbs started to stiffen. But when she closed her eyes, he stopped.

She opened them again quickly, and he picked up where he'd left off. So he wasn't kidding about keeping her eyes open. She didn't mind. As long as he kept doing what he did so well.

The buildup began again. Quick breaths, heat, muscles tightening—

He stopped.

"Hey," she protested.

"Patience."

"My ass."

"Oh, I like it when you talk dirty."

"Cole!"

He stepped back, and she didn't know was what was going to happen next.

He didn't make a move. Not a smile, not a gesture.

"Cole?"

"Yes?"

"Are we staring at each other for a reason?"

He nodded.

"Can I ask what that reason is?"

"You'll figure it out."

"Great. Puzzles. Just what I was hoping for."

He laughed out loud and it made her blush with pleasure. "It isn't a puzzle so much as a game. And it's your move."

"Ah," she said, the light dawning. "I see. Hmm." She tapped her lips with her finger, trying to hide the excitement that filled her with joy and power and a want as real as the one straining the buttons on Cole's Levi's.

Oh.

She took a couple of steps, just enough so that if she wanted to touch him, she could. But she didn't. Not yet. She wanted to get this right. Give as good as she'd gotten.

There was this thing she'd read about. It had always seemed a bit much. But given the circumstances? What the hell.

COLE WASN'T SURE he could keep this up. The waiting, that is. The gleam in her eyes told him his torment would end soon.

She put her hands on his belt and slowly pulled the leather through the loops until she held it in her hands. Then she walked behind him.

He started to turn, but her hand on his shoulder stopped him.

"Hmm."

"What?"

"Patience."

"Smart-ass."

She patted his butt. "That's me."

She took hold of his left wrist and pulled it in back of him. Then she wrapped his belt around it. Next, she got his other wrist, and that, too, she tied with the belt. She made a loop of the leather. He tugged. There was a little give, but not much.

No one had ever tied him up before. While one part of him hated it—hated not being in control—another part of him was almost too excited. If she touched him right now, he was afraid he wouldn't be able to hold back.

"Very intriguing, don't you think?" she whispered, her lips grazing his ear.

"Cute. But not that cute. Come on, Lily. Take it off."

"Patience, patience."

He gritted his teeth as she walked around him, trailing her fingers over his back, his arms, his chest. When she was in front of him again, her fingers moved straight down until she found his waistband.

She pulled him closer, yanking him by the pants. His automatic response was to stop himself, but of course, he couldn't. Another try at breaking free, testing the belt, met with failure.

She had the power, and all he could do was take what she might give. It was completely unsettling. No woman had ever dared try anything like this. He'd made it clear he liked to be in charge.

Until Lily.

Her fingers played along his fly, rubbing his erection through the denim. He shuddered, willing her to get on with it.

She undid his top button. He held his breath.

She undid the next button. He forced himself to stay calm.

She undid all the rest of the buttons. He nearly lost it.

Then her lips went to his chest. As she pushed down his jeans, she kissed him, licked him, leaving a hot, wet trail all the way down his stomach. She paused as she reached the crucial juncture in removing his clothes. She crouched down, her hands on his hips. He felt her lips on his stomach, just below his navel. Another shudder ran through him.

Then she carefully, slowly, pushed his jeans past the point of no return. Of course, Cole Junior sprang to attention. The feel of the air alone was enough to make him moan. And when she touched him with her fingertips, he bit his lower lip, hard, and thought of the pain instead of the pleasure.

She ran her hand all the way down to the base of him, then back to the head. He'd never been this hard, never been so ready. If only she would...

She did. He felt her lips encircle him, the shock of her warm tongue. It was agony. And ecstasy. He wanted to touch her, but the damn belt—

He couldn't believe what her mouth was doing to him. As much as he wanted to impress her with his staying power, he knew he couldn't last much longer. He wanted her too much.

As if sensing his imminent explosion, she stopped her ministrations. She stood up. Smiled at him in that devilish way of hers. Sliding his jeans the rest of the way down, she held them while he freed himself of their constraint. Then she went behind him again, grabbed his wrists and pulled him backward. He didn't want to go. At least not in this direction. The bed was over there, across the room. But she called the shots, and he took one step after another away from heaven. Finally, the back of his legs hit his chair, and she pushed him down. The leather of the oversize club chair was damn cold on some places that were mighty hot. She grinned at his gasp.

"You're a cruel woman, Lily Garrett."

She nodded. "Cruel and mean and just awful. I don't know what you see in me."

"Me, neither."

She took a couple of steps back. What a feast for his eyes. Her long hair, long legs, those incredible breasts. If she didn't hurry—

Her fingers went to her panties, and she made a show of taking them off, teasing him unmercifully with the movement of her hips. Maybe it was a good thing they hadn't gone right to the bed. Maybe he could calm himself down a little. The last thing he wanted was for things to be over in two seconds. He took a deep breath, which caught when she straightened and tossed her panties over her shoulder. She was magnificent. She didn't have much hair. She was mostly bare and smooth and as erotic a sight as he'd ever seen.

She approached him slowly. With each step, he got harder, which was damn near a miracle. So much for calming down. She didn't stop until her legs were against his knees. Then she put her hands on his shoulders, gave him a wicked smile, and lifted her leg, wedging her knee between his leg and the arm of the chair. Using him as a fulcrum, she climbed up so she straddled him.

He had to admit, it was interesting.

He leaned forward and kissed her just below her

breasts. Her scent, clean and womanly, made him curse his belt and her foolishness. He wanted her. Now.

As it happened, he got his wish.

She lowered herself inch by slow inch until his eyes were level with her breasts. Then one hand went from his shoulder to his penis, holding him steady as she continued down.

He couldn't do anything. The way she leaned on him made it impossible to even thrust up. "Lily, let me go."

"No."

"I said untie me, dammit."

"And I said no. Just relax."

He tried to free himself again. It was no use.

"Don't struggle," she whispered. "I promise, it will be okay."

"I—"

"Look at me."

He met her smoldering gaze. And as they stared into each other's eyes, she lowered herself those last inches. He'd never known he could feel this intensely.

She didn't move, even though he desperately wanted her to. But then her silken muscles flexed and released around him. No other part of her moved. She just squeezed him until he thought he'd go insane. Finally, when he couldn't stand it one more second, she rose up, then down, then up again.

She moaned and tossed her head back, her fingers tight on his shoulders. Faster now, taking him for the ride of his life. He struggled with his hands, struggled to move, to thrust, but he couldn't.

She rode him with complete abandon, with utter

control. Watching the ecstasy on her face, he stopped fighting. Stopped trying to make it happen his way. He let her lead him all the way to the most intense climax of his life.

earnest. Watching she pulled on her knob, he snapped lighting, stopped crying to watch it Instant his text To let her head huh all the way to the most intense climax of his life.

CHAPTER FIFTEEN

LILY SAGGED against him as she tried to slow her breathing. Now that she'd climaxed—oh *boy,* how she'd climaxed—her leg muscles rebelled against her unorthodox position.

What on earth had possessed her? She'd never been kinky. Well, okay, maybe a little kinky. But no whips or chains or anything. So why had she been so determined to tie Cole's hands?

His breathing was still in high gear, too. She needed to move, but he was still inside her and she didn't want to let him go. Of course, getting a charley horse wasn't exactly romance personified, so she grabbed his shoulders again and untangled herself from him and the chair. "Be right back," she said, then kissed him on the nose.

"Hey!"

"What?" she called over her shoulder as she hurried to the bathroom.

"I'm tied up here."

"I know." Then she slipped inside and closed the door behind her. She was asking for it. Oh, yes.

After she took care of the pressing issues, she slowed down as she faced the mirror. Naked as the day she was born, she looked like a woman who had just been most deliciously laid. Her hair was a mess, her lips swollen and red, and her chin and cheeks were pink with stubble burn. The very picture of the joy of sex.

It occurred to her that their sexual frenzy had made them both irresponsible. Thank goodness she was on the pill. At least she didn't have to worry about that.

Her mood a little flattened by that left turn to reality, she washed her face, brushed her hair, and headed back to free Cole.

Good night Irene, he *was* a gorgeous hunk of a man. Sitting in the altogether like that made her a wee bit itchy for round two. Only this time, she wanted his hands unfettered. Yum.

"Are you going to stand there all night, or are you going to untie me?"

"Now, now. Don't get testy."

"I'm not testy," he said, testily.

She moved to the back of the chair while he leaned forward. A few seconds later, she'd untied him, and he stood. While he rubbed his wrists, he looked at her through narrowed eyes. "Mind me asking you a personal question?"

She grinned. "What? You think what we just did wasn't personal?"

"My question is about that, actually."

"Oh, don't worry. I'm not normally that, uh, creative."

"No?"

"I never have been."

"Hmm."

"What's that look for?"

"Nothing."

"Cole. What is going on in that gorgeous head of yours?"

He walked around the chair until he was very close

to her. "It's not that I didn't like it," he said, his voice that husky whisper that sent chills up her spine. "I'm just used to playing a more active role."

"That was the point, silly."

"The point?"

She touched his cheek with her hand, loving the masculine feel of his beard, and beneath that the warmth of his skin. "It seemed the right thing to do. To take charge like that. To let you be on the receiving end."

"I don't like feeling helpless."

"But you're helpless all the time. So am I. So is everyone. There are things in life that we have no control over. But that doesn't mean we can't enjoy the experience."

"Odd time to make a philosophical point."

"I wasn't trying to make a point. I just went with what felt right. But now that I think about it, I understand why I did it."

"Because you wanted to teach me Buddhism?"

"Ha. My goal was as basic as it gets."

He nodded, although suspicion still darkened his eyes.

"Honest." She crossed her heart with her index finger. "I had only impure intentions."

"Okay. But next time—" He stopped midsentence. The suspicion in his gaze turned to worry.

"It's all right, cowboy. I know there isn't going to be a next time."

"I—"

"Well, maybe one more time. For heaven's sake, you just sat there like a lump. I think I deserve one go with you participating fully."

"Hey, wait just a damn minute."

She grinned. "I know it's early, but can I sleep over?"

He shook his head. "No. Absolutely not. We've already gone too far. I should never have touched you. I won't make that mistake again."

"Oh. Okay then." She turned to leave, but he stopped her with a touch. Searched her face with those dark, brooding eyes of his. Then he sighed. "I sleep on the right. And I don't like the windows open."

"You charmer. How could I ever resist?"

Taking her by the hand, he led her over to the bed, then pulled her into his arms. The feel of his naked body made her shiver.

"I can't resist," he whispered. "That's the whole problem."

"Let's make a deal, shall we?"

"What?" he asked, lowering her down to the cool sheets.

"How about if we pretend it isn't a problem, and declare a truce for tonight? Tomorrow, we can pick up our angst at the door."

"You're very strange."

"I know." She punctuated the short sentence by rubbing her hips against him. "But that's beside the point. Do we agree? No past, no future, no ifs, ands or buts. Just pleasure until the sun comes up."

"Very strange, and very beautiful." He kissed her tenderly, then nipped her lower lip. "But I have to admit, from time to time, you do have some inspired ideas."

Lily closed her eyes and let out a soft sigh as Cole's fingers trailed down her stomach.

Being with Cole was easy. So comfortable. The

only fly in the ointment was her lies, but she wouldn't think about that now. Not while his finger circled her belly button, then moved down her pelvis. When he reached the small patch of hair, he lingered there with a featherlight touch. She turned her head slightly on his big down-filled pillow, then grew still once more. The overhead fan sent waves of cool air over her body. It wasn't that the room was hot, but Cole was, and her body and his touched from shoulder to knee. He was on his side, she was on her back. It was perfect. "You know what?"

"What?"

She smiled. "You have wonderful hands." She felt the vibration of his chuckle against her arm.

"I know. Which is why tying them up was such a shame."

She looked at him. "Are you going to keep harping on that? Did you or did you not enjoy yourself?"

"Yes, I enjoyed myself. And no, I'm not going to harp on it. I'm just making the observation that this way can be enjoyable, too."

To illustrate the point, his sly fingers moved down to her soft, bare folds. He petted her as if she were a cat, and he damn near had her purring. But he also made her want him. It was all she could do to remain still. To stop herself from thrusting up, forcing his fingers to do more than pet.

"So soft," he whispered. "So beautiful."

She couldn't help herself. Her hips moved up slightly, just as his finger hovered over the most sensitive part of her body.

"So, that's how it is, eh?"

She nodded. "Oh, my, yes."

He dipped inside her, and continued his slow moves up and down the moist heat.

There was no way to stay still now. Her body fairly hummed with a desire that built and built.

His lips found her earlobe and he nipped the tender flesh, then he swirled his tongue in the soft shell, giving her goose bumps. But a moment later, those same lips captured her mouth in a kiss as gentle as the breeze.

She kissed him back, tenderly, sweetly. A long, languid exploration of taste and sensation. *What he did to her.* It was more than she could ever explain, more than she could even understand. He knew exactly how to kiss her without her saying a word. He touched her with magic fingers. He moved with a masculine grace that stoked a flame deep inside.

As he nibbled his way down her chin, it hit her. This was truly making love. And it was her first time.

His kiss deepened at the same time as his fingers. She moaned in contentment as he thrust into her, then in disappointment as he broke the kiss. But she didn't complain for long. His talented mouth rained kisses down her chin and between her breasts, down farther and farther until he had to shift his body so he could move between her legs.

His warm breath preceded his lips as he pleasured her. He explored every part of her most intimate self, finally centering on the one spot that would send her to the moon.

She gripped the bedsheets, but they didn't hold. As the tension mounted, she reached back and found purchase on the headboard. Her breathing grew faster and more urgent, her hips bucked, but the pressure never wavered. Harder. Faster. There, there, *there.*

Lily cried out as she went over the edge, as her body trembled and her muscles tensed.

Before she could relax, before the echoes of her climax had stilled, he was over her, his weight on his hands, his face above hers. He captured her gaze, and as his expression became a mask of intensity, he entered her. There was no hesitation, no pause. He filled her completely, and she cried out again. He moved with a steady, powerful rhythm, and with each thrust he rekindled her climax. As strong as the sensations were where they joined, they didn't compare with the passion of his gaze or the fire in his eyes. The desire there was so raw, so real she would have trembled without a touch.

It was more than making love. It was a melding of bodies, souls, spirits. There was no separation. No him and her, only them. Only this. Only now.

His eyes finally closed, but only for a moment. When he opened them again, his mouth curled into a grimace, his neck muscles bulged and he rocked the whole bed with his thrusts. He came with a primal cry that touched the deepest part of her heart.

A moment later, after he was drained and she had caught whatever breath she could, he lay down, wrapping his arms around her tightly. His breath and hers mingled, their chests rising and falling, the sheen on her body becoming the sheen on his.

She kissed him all over his face. His eyes, his nose, his lips, his cheeks. And then she let her head fall back on the pillow. Closing her eyes as she struggled back to sanity, she had a moment of perfect clarity.

Something strange was happening here. She was reluctant to call it by name. It was too soon for that.

But she knew that this was different. That Cole was different. She just might be in serious trouble here.

But how could she tell if this was the real thing? Was this what it felt like? This shivering want? This feeling of completion when he was inside her?

Looking at him made her want to cry. She longed to tell him everything. To confess her lie, to show him the road to forgiving his grandmother, to heal him. Heal them both. But if he knew the truth, he'd hate her. And without the truth, there was no hope for them.

How could things have gone so far so fast? There was danger here, for her heart and his. She had the horrible suspicion it would all come to a bitter end. To make matters infinitely worse, she knew that her betrayal was going to be the final straw for Cole. He'd finally lowered the walls around his heart, and tomorrow she'd deal him a killing blow.

Could he possibly believe she had only good intentions? Could he ever forgive her?

She knew the answer to that. Tears came to her eyes, and though she blinked and struggled to hold them back, they fell down her cheeks in fat, hot streams.

If this wasn't love, she didn't know what it was. And if it was love…

What an unbelievable tragedy.

CHAPTER SIXTEEN

THE FIRST THING Cole saw when he woke up was Lily's face. She was fast asleep, her black mane of hair wild on his pillow, her eyelashes brushing the tops of her cheeks, her skin pale and perfect in the early morning light.

What had he done?

She was so beautiful it made him ache. At some point the night before, they'd gotten up and fixed sandwiches to bring back to bed. And then they'd talked...and talked. The way Lily listened— He'd held back nothing. She made him feel safe.

He knew it was dangerous, believing in her like this, but he was tired of being suspicious. Of holding himself apart from everyone and everything.

Lily had given him a push out the door of his exile. She'd ruined his plans, changed his mind about how he would have his child. Dammit, he was in the exact position he'd wanted most to avoid. Being numb was easier. Shutting off his emotions ensured that he would never be hurt. He'd really blown it this time.

Why in hell had she come to his door? Even more puzzling was why he'd let her stay. He'd known right away she wasn't the right one to mother his child. At least, not the way he'd planned it.

Now he couldn't ignore the fact that he'd thought about having children with her. Lots of children.

They'd watch them grow together as a team. Loving them, and each other.

He wanted to touch her. To feel the warmth of her body, the silk of her skin. He wanted to know everything about her. And he wanted her to know everything about him.

So now what? Was he supposed to drop his plans just like that? Ask her to marry him for real? Or should he show her the door and forget he ever met her?

That last thing wouldn't be easy. She wasn't forgettable. Her humor, that sassy mouth of hers. The way her hair shimmered. And now... Oh, man, now he knew what it was to be inside her. To feel her lips on him. It wasn't enough. He wanted more. He could imagine doing everything with her. All his most private fantasies. She'd be game.

He wondered what she fantasized about? That would be interesting. And a little scary. She was so unpredictable. When she'd tied him up—

He felt himself harden as he remembered. It had frustrated him like crazy, but it had also excited him. She could have done anything to him and he wouldn't have been able to stop her. She could have hurt him. But she hadn't.

What was it she'd said? She wanted him to feel helpless. She'd told him he was helpless all the time. It was true, he supposed. He had no influence over the weather, the stock market, the men who worked for him. He was helpless to create the world he wanted, even though he'd sure as hell tried. So maybe she was right. Maybe the thing to do was relax and enjoy life. Let the chips fall where they may.

It would mean being vulnerable. But wasn't he,

anyway? He'd already gone past the point of no return. If she left him now, it would hurt. Hurt like crazy.

He hadn't known her long enough to be feeling these things. He'd known Carrie for months before he'd honestly cared for her. But Carrie had never been so open with him. She'd been guarded, and had made it easy for him to keep his thoughts to himself.

Not Lily. She'd press and intrude and annoy him until he told her everything. Was that a bad thing? He had no clue.

All he did know was that he'd made mistakes before, and he wasn't arrogant enough to think he wouldn't make them again. But some mistakes were worse than others.

He brushed her cheek with the back of his hand. She made him care too much. It was no use trying to kid himself. He'd let her inside. All he could do was pray that she hadn't brought any weapons with her. His heart wouldn't survive another assault.

LILY WOKE with a start. For a moment, she was still in the dream, still being punished by an unseen hand. But the dream dissipated as consciousness took hold. Cole wasn't next to her, and she didn't like that at all. She wanted the comfort of his arms.

She sat up and saw the light under the bathroom door. Heard the faint sound of his shower. Part of her wanted to rush to the bathroom and climb in the shower with him. Even though she was sore from last night, she still wanted him. Wanted him like she'd never wanted anything in her life.

What an ass she was! Such a selfish little weasel. She'd been so cocky, so sure she'd find a perfect solution to this problem and be back at the Double G in a couple of days, bringing Cole with her. A tearful reunion would follow, and she'd move on to the next case.

Right.

She was knee-deep in alligators, and it was her own fault. She'd screwed up big time, and she didn't know how to go about making things right.

She checked the door, listened carefully. The water was still running. She threw back the covers and found her clothes, dressing as she went along. When she had everything on except her boots, she tiptoed out the door and closed it behind her.

Dylan. Dylan would know what to do. He'd help her.

She hurried to her bedroom and closed, then locked the door. Dialing with shaky fingers, she said a small prayer that her brother was home. He was.

"Hey, it's me," she said.

"What's wrong?"

"Oh, everything."

"Want to start from the beginning?"

"Hold on a sec." She put the phone down, went into her bathroom, grabbed the box of tissues, then got the phone again. "I didn't mean for it to happen this way," she began.

"Of course you didn't. What way?"

She settled on the bed and told Dylan everything. No details about last night, of course, but the gist. She explained about Carrie, about his father and Eve. She assured him Cole wasn't a horrible man, just horribly hurt, and now she was going to have to hurt him again.

Dylan didn't interrupt. She heard him turn off his

computer halfway through her tale, and she could picture him as he sat at his desk. He'd be doodling, of course. He always did when he was on an important phone call. Nothing recognizable except for shapes. No names or eyes or little hearts.

She grabbed a tissue from the box and wiped her damp eyes. She felt like pond scum. Worse. "Dylan, what am I going to do? I've messed everything up so badly."

"You couldn't know it would turn out like this."

"But even so, I shouldn't have lied."

"He would have sent you packing the first five minutes."

"Then I should have been clever enough to find a way to make him listen."

"Oh, I see what we're doing."

"What?"

"I believe it's called self-flagellation. You don't need me for that."

She sighed as she scooted back on the bed, going right into the corner, taking her pillow with her. "Come on. Help me."

"I'm trying to. But you have to stop beating yourself up first."

"I don't know if I can."

"Look, kiddo, there's only one thing you can do, and I don't have to tell you what it is."

"Yes, you do."

"Fine. I'll spell it out. You have to tell him the truth."

"About Eve?"

"About everything."

"But—"

"Lily."

She closed her mouth, trying like heck to quiet all the justifications running through her head. "Go on."

"You have to tell him. He'll be angry. Who wouldn't be? But you've been there long enough for him to get to know you. He'll calm down eventually, and then he'll see the position you were in. He may not like it, but from what you've told me, he's a pretty smart guy. He'll see you didn't act maliciously."

"Will he?"

"I hope so, hon. But even if he doesn't, you still have to fess up."

"I don't know if I'm strong enough."

"You are."

"But—"

"Lily, you can. It'll be bad, but in the end you'll be glad you did it. You're not the kind of person who can live with lies. You never have been."

Her tears flowed in earnest now, blinding her, and making it hard to breathe. "Oh, Dylan."

He was quiet for a long moment. "You love him that much?"

Of course. She should have known he would guess. "More than that."

"More than Jason?"

She laughed bitterly. "In one of life's more ironic twists, my being here with Cole has made me very clear about my relationship with Jason. He was a jerk and I was obsessed and love never entered the picture."

"Are you sure?"

"I am now."

"Oh, man."

"You got that right. I'm well and truly screwed, little brother."

"I wish I could do more."

"I'm just glad you're there. Hold on." She put the phone down, wiped her eyes and blew her nose. She was able to breathe a little better when she picked up the cell phone. "So what's going on with you? Anything new?"

IN THEIR MAKESHIFT office at the ranch, Dylan stared at his desk pad. There was hardly a blank space left. He'd have to get a new one. It was impossible for him to sit quietly while on the phone. He was too antsy. "No, nothing new. Nothing but one dead end after another."

"Damn."

"Sebastian wanted to know if I thought we should call the investigation off."

"Are you kidding?"

"No. He's really disheartened. I know he's lost faith."

"What about you?"

"I'm not throwing in the towel. Just because I haven't found something yet doesn't mean I won't find the key tomorrow."

"Good for you."

He picked up the top sheet of his desk pad and crumpled it into a ball. After he'd scored by tossing it in the round file, he picked up his pen again. But he froze when he saw what he'd uncovered. A picture. He didn't remember putting it there, but he sure as hell remembered taking it.

Julie hadn't known. She'd been on her sundeck, soaking up some rays. He wasn't sure, but he thought she might have been asleep. Her hair glowed like a halo and the sun on her skin made her seem otherworldly. He'd been completely captivated. Totally smitten.

"Uh, Dylan? Did you fall asleep?"

He shook himself out of the memory. "No. I just got distracted for a minute. But I do have to get going. I've got an interview in a few minutes."

"Really?"

"You might know her. She's done a lot of volunteering for the Texas Fund for Children. Her name is Carolyn St. Clair."

"I may have heard the name, but no face is coming to mind. But that's good about her volunteering. I like that."

"I've got my fingers crossed."

"I guess I'll hang up then."

"You'll do great, Lily. It's a rough start, but hey, don't all great love stories start that way?"

She chuckled, which sounded odd with her stuffed nose. Dylan hoped Cole Bishop was a smart man. Because a smart man would see that she was a keeper. "Bye."

He hung up the phone as his gaze went back to the picture of Julie. It had been so long ago. Her hair had been short, and she'd thought it made her look too young. He'd thought it made her look beautiful. But then, he'd been in love.

Why hadn't he done something about it? He'd waited, and then it was too late. He'd shared all his hopes and dreams with her, but Sebastian was the one she had loved.

It was a sort of cruel torment to have remained friends all these years. But how could he justify ending his friendship? So he'd gone to Dallas and lost himself in the lives of other people. He'd become someone else, but the real kicker was that he'd still loved her. Even when he barely remembered his own name, Julie had been there. In his thoughts, in his heart.

A knock on the door startled him and he shoved the picture in the folds of the desk pad. The next time he ran across it, Julie would be home. At her home, with her husband. But that was okay. He'd had a long talk with God, and he'd promised that if Julie was safe, he'd never again begrudge Sebastian his happiness. "Come in."

A tall slender woman walked into the office. She was in her twenties, and she was a stunner. Her hair was almost red, but still brown, and it came down to her chin. He liked her immediately.

"Dylan Garrett, I presume?"

He rose and extended his hand. They shook, and he liked the feel of her, too. "Sorry about the office. We're still building the real thing, but it'll be a while longer yet." He indicated the chair by Lily's desk. "Have a seat. Can I get you coffee?"

"That would be great, thank you." She smoothed her slim green skirt and sat down, adjusting the matching jacket before she looked at him again. Her shoes and her purse were the same color. "I only had one cup this morning. Definitely not enough."

"I agree." He went to the pot and got a cup. "How do you take it?"

"Black is fine."

"Fair enough." As he poured her cup and another for himself, he realized he'd already made his decision. Unless the woman couldn't read or had a criminal record, she was it. The assistant he'd had in mind. "So tell me about yourself?"

"I live here in San Antonio. Have all my life. I've been working as an executive assistant for a law firm, but frankly, I'm looking for something a little less formal, if you know what I mean."

He brought the mugs and set them down, then took his seat across from her. "I do. What else appeals to you about this job?"

"I've always thought it would be terribly exciting to work for a private eye."

"You have?"

She nodded. "Yes." Her cheeks pinked a bit, and she had to clear her throat. "I think I'd be good at it, too. I like the details. The little puzzles. I've got one of those brains, you know. I think they call them helicopter brains."

"I don't know the expression."

She took a tentative sip of coffee, then raised her eyebrows with pleasure. "Nice, thank you. Anyway, there are people who have train brains, who follow logical steps from A to B to C. And then there are helicopter brains, who make connections from seemingly random events. Not to imply I can't go from A to B, if it's required."

"That's odd."

She got a panicky look on her face. "What?"

"I understood that."

Her smile sealed the deal.

"You do realize there's going to be computer input, filing, that kind of dull, mindless work."

"Of course. But I'm hoping there'll also be enough interesting work to offset it."

"I think there will be."

"Good."

"So when can you start?"

"Seriously?"

He nodded. "I'll have to check out your references, of course, but if there aren't any curve balls, the job is yours." He told her about the pay, the benefits, working with Lily. Enough information for her to make an informed decision.

When he finished she held out her hand. "I can't thank you enough, Mr. Garrett."

"Dylan," he said, taking her hand. "My father is Mr. Garrett. And he lives here, too. Along with Lily, of course, and the ranch foreman, Max Santana."

"Wow. Sounds lively."

"A little too lively sometimes."

"I can handle it."

He leaned back in his chair, well pleased. She would be able to handle it. And whatever else came her way. He knew it as surely as he knew his own name. Now, if only Lily's problem could be solved so handily...

CHAPTER SEVENTEEN

THE LONG DAY was coming to an end, and for Cole, it couldn't come a moment too soon. He'd forgotten all about his appointment with Jeff Harcourt until he'd shown up at the house. Harcourt was from *The Cattlemen*, and he was doing an article for the monthly trade paper. It was a damn shame Cole hadn't been able to focus properly. The article would surely make him look like a fool.

But he'd done the best he could, considering Lily was waiting for him. If he'd had his way, Cole would have spent the day out by the spring, thinking. Everything was topsy-turvy in his head.

He shook Harcourt's hand, then watched him get into his blue sedan. Once the car had disappeared down the road, Cole headed out for the barn. He wanted to see Lily something awful, but he needed some time. Time to figure out what was next.

He passed Spence, who looked at him curiously. "Aren't you going in to dinner?"

"I'll be there shortly."

Spence shrugged as he went toward the house.

Cole kept walking. Past the barn, past the paddock. He found himself in a copse of oaks, with streams of light peeking in between the leaves. He settled himself on a fallen log, and put his elbows on his knees.

He closed his eyes, listening to a faraway airplane, and then it was just the breeze rustling the leaves.

Things had changed. He hadn't wanted them to, but there it was. She'd been the catalyst, but he'd kept walking after she pushed.

In the shower this morning, when she lay sleeping in his bed, he'd realized he couldn't carry out his plan. He wasn't going to buy himself a son. Not that he couldn't, but he knew now that if he did, he was just asking for more heartache than he could stand.

She was right about that. He couldn't control another human being. Not through money or words or with his hands. All he could do was give his son the best that he had, and whatever the boy did with it after that, well, Cole would have to accept it. No matter what.

It would help if his son had a mother who was strong, intelligent, courageous. Who saw the humor in things. *Lily.* Any child would be lucky to have her for a mother. He'd be lucky to have her for a wife.

The thought nearly rocked him from the log.

He sat up straight, ran a hand over his face. How was it possible he wanted to ask this woman to be his wife? He hadn't known her long enough, and besides, he hadn't even called the detective to hear what he'd found out in his background check. Only a damn fool would want to marry a woman he'd only known for a few days.

He stood up, anxiety making him walk again. This was nuts. He didn't love her. He couldn't. It was too soon. And she was too much of an unknown.

But if he didn't love her, why was the thought of her leaving tearing at him? Why hadn't he hired Mrs.

Holt? She would have been perfect, yet he'd sent her away.

Lily had made him crazy. Certifiable. Making love with her had been a huge mistake. If he'd sent her home yesterday, he would have wondered what it would have been like. As it was, he knew. And that was worse. Much worse.

He'd never felt like this before. Never felt so calm and so excited, all at the same time. He'd never known making love could be so powerful. Before Lily, he'd enjoyed sex. He was a normal man with normal needs, after all. What he hadn't understood was that it could be so much more than physical.

Cole was no philosopher, and he didn't go in for any touchy-feely psychobabble, but dammit, he'd felt something in his soul last night. He'd found what had been missing all his life. He'd found it in her arms. In her body.

But he also didn't want to go off half-cocked. There was plenty of time to see how things would shake down. He didn't have to ask her to marry him or anything that radical. He just wouldn't hire a new cook, that's all. Then he'd see. He'd use his head for once. Think things through.

Good. He felt much better now that he had a course of action. He headed back to the house. He was as hungry as a bear. That's why he was walking so fast. Not because he'd get to see her.

Yeah, right.

LILY FORCED HERSELF to eat a little of the pot roast, but her stomach wasn't happy about it. In fact, her whole body was miserable, especially her heart.

Of course Cole knew something was wrong. All

through the meal he kept sending her these little looks. She'd smiled, trying not to make him worry. She failed at that, too.

Then Manny asked her if everything was all right. She nodded. And burst into tears. Completely unwilling to fall apart in front of everyone, she left the table and hurried to her bedroom. She heard Cole's chair scrape behind her.

Oh, God. This was it. This was the end. She had to tell him now, and see the expression on his face when he realized what kind of a horrible person she was. How she'd lied and manipulated—

She flung herself on the bed and buried her face in the pillow. He'd never reconcile with Eve now, and it was all her fault. She'd botched everything. And the worst of it was that she'd probably ruined Cole's chances of ever finding real love.

She still wasn't sure if she loved him. Everything was so confusing that she couldn't trust her emotions. But she was sure that leaving tonight was going to be terribly difficult.

She'd busted her butt all day, cooking meals for the freezer so Cole wouldn't have to worry for the next few days about hiring a cook. That had been awful, but not half as bad as packing had been.

Her suitcase was in the closet, ready to go. As she was. Damn ugly room. She should feel happy that at least she got to go back to the Double G. She'd get to help Dylan find Julie, and that was a good thing, right?

The knock on the door made her stomach churn. If only there was a way not to tell him the truth. To just leave and never look back.

Coward. She'd made this bed. And now she had to make Cole lie in it.

She got up, wiped her eyes with the backs of her hands, and went to the door. Her hand even found the doorknob. But it took an act of will that was quite nearly beyond her to turn it.

The look of concern on Cole's face started her crying all over again. He pulled her into his arms and held her tight, rocking her back and forth. She didn't even pretend to struggle. Instead, she put her head on his shoulder, wept like a child, and wished for a miracle. Between sobs, she inhaled deeply, knowing this was going to be the last time she'd be this close. She memorized the feel of his chest, the way his arms circled her body, the strength of him. She'd recognized that from the beginning. But then she'd thought it was purely physical. Now she understood how strong Cole really was. How hard he'd worked to become the man his father should have been.

"Honey, what is it?" he whispered. "Did I do something wrong?"

She leaned back. "No. You didn't do anything. It's me. It's all me."

He looked at her with his worried eyes, the furrow between his brows deep, his lips curved in a frown. So beautiful. The best-looking man she'd ever seen in the flesh. She sniffed, knowing it was time. She couldn't put it off any longer.

"Nothing can be that bad, honey," he said.

She closed her eyes for a moment, mustering all her courage. "Yes, it can. I need to talk to you Cole. And I need you to listen to the whole thing."

Cole let her take his hand as she led him to the bed. She stood as he sat, and from the way she paced, he had a sinking feeling this wasn't the female trouble he'd first imagined. This was serious.

She sniffed again, grabbed some tissue from a box by the bed, blew her nose, then stood in front of him. Her shoulders were back and her head held high, but he could tell she was damn nervous. What in hell?

"Cole, I—"

"What?"

Her face paled right in front of him. In fact, he thought she might pass out, but she didn't. She cleared her throat, touched her diamond necklace the way he'd seen people touch a cross and spoke again. "Cole, I came here under false pretenses."

The vague feeling of foreboding shifted into something far more concrete. Damn it all to hell. It *had* been too good to be true.

"I'm not a secretary at Finders Keepers. I'm one of the investigators. And I was hired by your grandmother."

"What?" His grandmother? What the—

"Eve is very ill, Cole. And she hates what's come between you. She wants to see you before she dies. She wants to say she's sorry."

Cole stood up and walked to the other side of the bedroom. He couldn't look at Lily right now. Not when he felt this kind of anger boiling inside him. He couldn't be sure what he'd do.

It had all been lies. His family had done it again. Only this time they'd hired the woman who would stab him in the back. The only thing missing was Lily telling him she was pregnant.

"Cole?"

"Your timing is off, Lily. If you'd waited a while,

I probably would have asked you to marry me. And then you could have had a really big laugh."

He heard her gasp, then the bed frame squeaked. When he turned, she was on the bed, her head in her hands, her shoulders shaking with her sobs. His first reaction was to go to her. To comfort her. Then he remembered. "You're good," he said. "I've got to give you that. I believed you."

She looked at him, her eyes red-rimmed and filled with shame. "I came here to do something noble. To try to help you and Eve make peace. I only lied because I didn't believe you'd listen to me."

"It would have been nice if you'd given me a chance."

She stood up. "Come on, Cole. I'm not trying to justify my actions, but you and I both know if I'd said Eve's name that first day, you would have booted me right out."

"And now I'm supposed to be grateful? I told you what she did. You know, and you can still ask me to see her?"

"People make mistakes. Even people you love. She loves you, Cole. She doesn't want to die with this bad blood between you."

"She should have thought of that when she paid off Carrie."

Lily sighed, then sniffed. "I don't want you to feel guilty," she said. "Later. When time has gone by, and Eve is gone."

"I won't feel guilty. I won't feel anything."

"Now you're the one who's lying. I know better. I know you feel everything. Too much. You were hurt, Cole, but now it's time to end it. To at least listen to her."

"Why? She'll just lie. Everyone does. Oh, she'll say the ends justify the means, but it'll still be a pack of lies."

Lily winced. "Don't blame her for my mistake. I should have done this better. I didn't know how."

"So you figured the best way to go about it was to climb in my bed? That as soon as you spread your legs I'd agree to anything?"

She jerked back as if he'd slapped her. "You can't believe I made love to you for that."

"I can. And I do. You forget, I've had a lot of experience with women like you. Women who use the bedroom to get what they want." He slammed a hand against the wall but it did no good. The rage was just as strong. "I can't believe I fell for it again. After I swore I wouldn't. After I built my entire life to protect myself from women like you."

"Cole—" She put her hand on his shoulder and he jerked away.

"Don't."

"Cole, I know I've hurt you. But I promised myself I would tell you everything, and so I'm going to."

"There's more?"

She nodded.

"Go on. Make my day."

She wept a little more, wiped her eyes with the crumpled tissue, then looked at him again. "The thing is, I didn't plan it this way. I never meant to— Oh, Cole. I think...I'm pretty sure...that I'm in love with you."

Cole felt as if a knife had been plunged into his chest. She was worse than anything he could have imagined. She made Carrie look like a Girl Scout.

"I'd be obliged if you would be gone by morning," he said, struggling to keep his voice calm.

"But—"

He didn't want to hear one more thing out of her mouth. He threw open the door and walked out. He kept on walking. Out of the house, out to the barn. He saddled Phantom and then he took off. He wasn't sure where he was going. He didn't give a damn. He just needed to get the hell away from Lily and her lies. Damn her for making him feel again. Damn her to hell.

LILY WASHED HER FACE, then folded her towel and put it back on the rack. Nothing of hers was left in the bathroom, or in the bedroom. It was as if she'd never been there.

She turned off the light and got her purse and her suitcase. The emptiness and ache inside her made walking difficult, made breathing difficult. She'd done so much damage. Hurt him so badly. She deserved everything she'd gotten.

But that didn't make leaving any easier. So much had affected her in the short time she'd been here. The guys. Manny with his cursing and his love for the work and Rita. Chigger, such a courtly gentleman, so sweet. J.T., Spence, John. They'd all treated her with complete respect and offered their friendship freely, no strings attached. She'd miss them. Miss the talk at the table, the jokes, the compliments about her cooking.

She turned off the light in the barren little bedroom and headed down the hall. Cole wasn't in the house. No one was. She would leave in the dark, without a word, in shame. It fit. There should be no tearful goodbyes. She'd lied to them all.

In the living room, she stopped and let her gaze travel over the drab furniture, the unadorned walls. She'd decorated the place in her mind. Several times, in fact. While she'd been cooking, she'd put some paintings on that wall, added a rug, brought in some plants.

The tears threatened again, and she couldn't let that happen. She'd cried too much tonight, and she had a long drive ahead of her. Besides, there would be many, many more opportunities to weep after she was home.

She walked out the door, closing it behind her. Closing it for the last time. Leaving her heart behind as she headed to her car.

CHAPTER EIGHTEEN

COLE TURNED OFF his computer and headed toward the kitchen. Mrs. Holt was making pork chops tonight, and he'd always been fond of them. She was a good cook, everything her résumé had promised. But she wasn't Lily.

The two weeks since she'd left had been hell. The work got done, and the bills got paid, and the sun rose and set, but Cole wasn't part of it.

None of the men had asked him what happened. They never even said her name. Which was good. Now, if he could just get her out of his head, things might have a chance of getting back to normal.

He'd given up his dream to have a child. No more searching, no more planning. He understood and accepted that he had no judgment when it came to women. No radar that told him good from bad, lies from truth. He couldn't trust himself worth spit.

The thing he regretted the most was making love with her. Sleep had become a rare commodity. She plagued him in his dreams. The memory of her body, of her kisses, of her scent snuck up on him and made his insides tighten with hurt and want. Crazy, huh? That he still wanted her. After everything she'd told him. It made no sense.

He'd thought a lot about his grandmother, too.

About when he'd been a kid, playing in that big old house of hers. How she'd slip him hard candy when his mother wasn't looking. How she'd listen to him for hours as she sat at her secretary, writing notes and grocery lists, paying bills. She never chased him out of the room. Not like his father had.

He'd be the first to admit there had been good times. But that didn't change the way things had gone down. Eve had hurt him almost as much as his father had. What more was there to say?

He supposed there was one good thing that had changed since Lily had left. He'd stopped blaming Eve. He'd stopped blaming anyone but himself. He'd come to see the pattern of his life, and he'd figured out how to deal with it. Everyone he'd loved had betrayed him, so he wouldn't love anyone. Simple. Clean. Safe. He'd keep to himself. And his men. He'd work. He might even try his hand at writing some articles. But he'd never expect anything again. Not from another living soul.

So what if there was no laughter at the dinner table? It didn't matter at all that the silence of the night drove him crazy. He'd adjust. In time, the ache would leave. The want would stop. It had to.

COLE DIDN'T MEAN TO SPY. He was just rinsing out a glass at the kitchen sink when he saw Manny dressed up in a suit and tie, his hair combed, his shoes shined, looking like a man on his way to the chapel. Which wasn't that far off. A moment later, his girl Rita was heading toward him, and she, too, was dressed to the nines. Her long dark hair swayed down her back, and her dress, a soft blue, clung to her body in a way that would make any man swallow hard. The way they looked at each other...

His fingers hurt and he glanced down to see that he was squeezing the glass so hard it was about to shatter. He put it down, determined not to look out the window again. But he did. He watched Manny touch Rita's hair, a tender caress. Then they kissed, and a pain like fire lit up in Cole's chest.

He had no business envying Manny. Wishing things could have been different. But...

Damn, it had been three weeks since she'd left. He should have felt better by now. He should have stopped dreaming about her every blessed night.

The thing that kept gnawing at him was remembering that first day. How he'd been talking on the phone while she stood there looking so beautiful it took his breath away. He'd had to consciously harden his heart and his voice so she wouldn't suspect what she'd done to him just by showing up.

If she'd brought up Eve that afternoon, if she'd told him the truth about why she was there, he knew for a fact he would have shown her the door. He wouldn't have listened to another word.

It didn't excuse the lies. Or did it? He wasn't sure anymore. He wasn't sure about much. Only that he missed her. And that his life felt as empty as the walls of his house.

Manny took Rita's hand, and they walked off toward their car. Cole watched until they disappeared from view. He tried to work up his anger, to hide in his self-righteousness. It didn't work. He didn't have the energy anymore.

She'd been wrong to lie. But maybe, just maybe, she hadn't meant to hurt him.

LILY KNEW something was wrong. Not just with her emotions, but with her body. And it terrified her to think what it might be.

It was almost a month since she'd walked out of Cole Bishop's life. The worst month she could ever remember. Dylan had helped. He'd been wonderful these last weeks. Really a sweetheart. He hadn't said a word about her crying fits, or her dour mood. He'd been patient and kind, and he'd tried his best to make her feel better. But he knew there was nothing in heaven or earth that would fix the hurt inside her. Time, they said. But what did they know?

She opened the paper bag from the pharmacy and pulled out the package. A home pregnancy test. Just looking at it made her knees weak, and she sat down on the edge of her bed.

She'd been on the pill. She couldn't be pregnant. She hadn't missed taking any, not one. The only reason she thought she might, just *might* be…was because of an article she'd read about drug interactions. It seemed the kind of antibiotics she'd taken could sometimes lessen the effectiveness of birth control pills. She could hardly see the scar on her hand from that dog bite. It didn't seem possible.

But she was two weeks late. She'd never been late before. And dammit, she couldn't stop crying. It was ridiculous. Anything set her off—commercials, movies, even a tender word. She'd just get to weeping and sometimes it felt as though she would never stop.

Of course, the work had suffered. If it hadn't been

for Carolyn, everything would have gone to hell in a hand basket. She'd been great, never prying, but always willing to listen. Lily was lucky. Her whole family supported her, tried to convince her that this mess wasn't her fault. But she knew better.

She kept remembering the look on Cole's face. The hurt, the disbelief, and finally, the rage. As icing on the cake, she also had the memory of Eve's disappointment lodged in her brain. Eve had said it was all right, that Lily shouldn't blame herself, but that was just kindness talking. There was no one else to blame, and everyone knew it.

It was no use putting this off any longer. She had to know.

She hadn't let herself think about what she would do if the test was positive. Of course, she would keep the child. There was no question about that. But her secret shame that she could barely own up to herself, let alone talk about with her brother or sister, or anyone, was that part of her wanted to be carrying his child. It wasn't right, and she had no business thinking about it, but she couldn't help it.

It would be part of Cole. That alone made her hope for a plus sign on the indicator. Could she possibly be any more selfish? No. She'd reached the apex, the absolute summit of self-centeredness. She wanted this baby, even though she knew how it would wound Cole. In his eyes she'd be just like Carrie. But the thought of not having even a part of him made the rest of her life seem such a lonely proposition.

She got up and walked slowly to the bathroom. Locking herself in, she read the directions and went about the rather undignified process of finding out what her future was going to hold.

COLE COULD HARDLY believe he was standing on his grandmother's doorstep. Just driving up to the place had filled him full of conflicting emotions. The good times—damn, there had been so many—overshadowed by a depth of betrayal he didn't even know how to express.

Maybe this was a mistake. He should just turn around. Go back to his new life, his safe life. But how could he? Lily had changed everything. She'd told him things he didn't want to know. Like the fact that Eve was sick. Dying.

He'd sworn never to speak to her again, so why was he here? What did he hope to accomplish? That was the thing. He didn't know. Did he honestly think he would find peace here? That he'd learn how to sleep again? To stop beating himself up for every decision he'd ever made? Was it as simple as seeing his grandmother?

Simple, but not easy. Years of anger held his hand at his side, instead of letting him knock on the door. How large these doors had been as a child. The whole house had seemed gigantic, full of places to hide and places to explore. He'd loved it here, once.

Despite his misgivings, he knocked. Maybe no one would answer. Then he could go home, knowing he'd tried his best. He waited, his heart pounding hard in his chest, his hands damp, but not from the humid air. No one came to the door after five seconds, ten seconds.

He knocked again after a full two minutes.

This time, the door swung open. A woman he didn't know smiled at him.

"Can I help you?"

He almost said no. "I'm here to see Eve Bishop."

"Is she expecting you?"

He shook his head. "I doubt it."

"Your name?"

The woman was attractive and, oddly, barefoot. Things had certainly changed around here if the help didn't need to wear shoes. "I'm her grandson. Cole."

Her eyes widened and her mouth dropped open in an almost comic double take. He might have laughed if he could've found anything funny about it.

"Come in, Mr. Bishop," she said, stepping back quietly so he could get by her. "Oh, she'll be so happy. Stay here, please. One moment." She hurried down the hall, but stopped after ten feet. "Please, wait." Then she turned and ran.

Cole wasn't going anywhere. Not yet. He'd come this far, he wasn't going to back out now. But that didn't mean everything was going to be all hunky-dory with Eve. The facts hadn't changed. No matter how old she got, how sick, she had done what she had done.

His gaze fell on an old pitcher atop a mahogany console table. They had both been there all his life. Nothing fancy or ornate, but simple and elegant. His grandmother's taste in a nutshell.

A wave of nostalgia hit him hard, and a hundred images fought for preeminence in his mind. The smell of the soap in the downstairs bath. The sound of tennis shoes on the white marble. His mother's laughter drifting down the staircase.

If only—

"Mr. Bishop."

He looked up to see the maid standing by the library door.

"Please."

He started across the foyer, and every step brought more memories. And more tension to his gut. He paused as he reached the door, knowing it was his last chance to make a clean break. And then he walked into his grandmother's favorite room.

Everything looked the same. The dolls, the portrait, the carpet, the lace doilies. Everything but Eve. She'd gotten so old. So frail. Seeing her holding on to her cane, tears spilling over her wrinkled, nearly translucent skin, propelled him forward. He needed to touch her. To make sure she was real. To stop time.

"My baby," she whispered. "My Cole."

He wrapped her in his arms, forcing himself not to squeeze too hard. She was so tiny. Like a little bird. His eyes burned and he blinked the heat away, then stepped back to really look at her.

Her eyes had paled, but her strength was still there. Her determination, her courage. And her stubbornness. "Hi, Grandma."

She smiled, and it lit up her face. "Lily said—"

He nodded. "I know. I wasn't going to come. But I figured it was time we did some talking."

She stepped back and ushered him to the couch. After he sat, she did, too, although with her it took a shaky moment. Finally, she was in her wing chair, her white hair pulled up on her head, her cardigan sweater buttoned and her cane resting on the cushion. He wondered how long it would be until the maid brought tea. Eve had always been crazy about tea time.

He didn't have to wait long. Even before either one of them could figure out how to begin, the door opened, and the barefoot woman brought in a tray. The next few minutes were devoted to the old ritual. Eve remembered how he liked his tea. Well, how he drank it. He was a coffee man, but he wouldn't complain today.

She handed him his cup.

His gaze followed the maid until she left the room and closed the door. "That's different," he said.

"Angie? She's very nice. Patient."

"I remember when the help had to wear uniforms."

His grandmother smiled ruefully. "One of the advantages of growing old is that foolish notions can be left by the wayside."

"It really doesn't bother you that she doesn't wear shoes?"

"No. It doesn't. She hates shoes. But she always offers to wear them when company is coming. I don't insist. If her bare feet offend, well, then, that's too bad. Angie has made my life bearable these last few years. I don't know what I would have done without her."

Cole felt shame rise in his gullet. His own flesh and blood had to be taken care of by a stranger. But then, hadn't Eve done that to herself? Hadn't her actions dictated the outcome?

She studied him with her pale eyes, focusing on her face. "You look more like your mother now."

"Do I?"

She nodded. "But I see your father in you, too."

He didn't like the comparison. "I'm nothing like him."

"No, I suppose you're not. I assume you want to talk about what happened."

She never was one to beat around the bush. And neither was he. "Yes, I do."

"It was a sorry mess," she said. "A tragedy of selfishness and greed."

He put his cup down, not at all sure he could keep his hands steady enough not to spill the hot liquid all over her couch. "It didn't have to end badly between us."

"Cole, I did what I did because I loved you. I didn't want to see you in any more pain."

He opened his mouth, but he stopped himself before the torrent of vitriol escaped. After a deep breath to compose himself, he asked her the question that had bothered him for five years. "How could you possibly believe I wouldn't want my child? No matter what Carrie did, it wasn't the boy's fault. There was no excuse for terminating the pregnancy. None."

Eve's lips quivered, but instead of falling apart, she sat up straighter. "I didn't realize you knew about that."

"I got a letter from Carrie. She told me you paid for everything. A nice tidy ending for a messy business."

"I did use my money to get rid of her, and I'm not sorry for it. Not a bit. She was a convincing one. Playing you against your father like that. It still makes me angry."

"But that doesn't justify—"

She held up her hand. "I have very real doubts that what Carrie told you was the truth."

"You just admitted as much."

"I admitted to paying her to disappear and never come back."

"And the child?" Cole's hands were wet, and his head pounded with the worst headache he'd had in years. What compelled him to hear the details? Couldn't he just let it go?

"I'm sorry to have to be the one to tell you this. I would have thought Carrie would. She was looking for ways to hurt you, and this would have been the capper."

"What are you talking about?"

She looked away for a moment, up to the portrait of herself as a young woman. Then she faced him, met his gaze. "The child wasn't yours, Cole."

"What?"

"The child wasn't your son. He was your brother."

He knew the instant the words were out of her mouth that she was telling the truth. Holy god, he'd known it somehow, on some level. It wasn't his child. It had never been his child.

"And for the record," Eve said, her voice a raggedy whisper, "I didn't know she was going to use the money to have an abortion. She'd agreed to give the child up for adoption. I found out after."

He tried to think of something to say, but his thoughts were too jumbled. What struck him hardest was the waste. The waste of a new life, the waste of his love, and the waste of all those years he'd spent in anger. He'd blamed everyone for his stupidity, and he'd focused his hurt on the one person who had never shown him anything but love.

"I'm so grateful I got to tell you these things before I die."

"You're not—"

"Yes, I am. But not today. Today I get to visit with my grandson. I get to hear all about his life. I get to put my hand on his arm. I'm very lucky, don't you think?"

He rose on unsteady feet and crossed to the big wing chair that held the small woman sitting so tall, and he got down on his knees in front of her. He took her wrinkled, delicate hands in his own and he kissed her. "I'm such a fool."

"No," she said. "We all made mistakes. You were hurt. I knew that. I should have found you then. Made sure you understood. But I was stubborn."

"I can't believe that everything I've thought for all these years—"

"It's all right," she said, moving her hand to cup his cheek. "The important thing is that you came. That you're here now. That you've given me a chance. Bless Lily Garrett."

At the mention of Lily's name, Cole rose.

"She didn't think you would come," Eve said.

He nodded. "I wasn't going to."

"What changed your mind?"

He went back to the couch and sat down again, still reeling from the earthquake that had shaken his righteous anger. "She did. She made me think about things I'd been too stubborn to face. She changed everything."

A slow smile lit Eve's face. "She did, did she?

Well, why don't we heat up that tea of yours while you tell me how.''

THE PHONE CALL had come a week after Lily had taken the test. Eve had asked to see her. There had been no explanation, just the simple request. Lily had, of course, said she'd come. But now that she was at the old mansion, she hesitated before getting out of her car.

So much had happened. So much she didn't understand. Big questions remained, and she was trying her best to figure out how to handle it all.

Her hand went to her stomach. She wasn't showing at all yet. In fact, if she hadn't gone to the doctor and had it verified, she hardly would have believed it. Cole's baby was inside her, and these last few days she'd been struggling to decide how to tell him.

She'd left two phone messages, but he'd never called her back. She supposed she didn't blame him. If he didn't call her back by the weekend, she'd have to go out to his ranch. Perhaps that was the best course anyway. This was the kind of news that needed to be given in person.

She got out of the car and climbed the steps to the door. A few moments later and she was once again following the barefoot maid to the library. Eve had the tea service on the cart next to her chair.

''Come in, Lily.''

As Lily moved closer, she noticed a subtle difference in the older woman. A shine to her eyes, and some pink in her cheeks. No sign at all of her stroke, except perhaps a slight droop on the left side of her mouth. ''You look wonderful.''

"I'm feeling well, thank you."

"I'm glad." Lily kissed her cheek, then sat across from her. "And I'm glad you asked me to come by."

"Good." Eve poured, remembering how Lily took her tea. "I want to ask you some questions, if you don't mind."

"Of course not."

She handed Lily her cup and saucer, then folded her weathered hands on her lap. "I'd like to know what happened between you and my grandson."

Lily put her cup down quickly, wondering what she should say. "I'm not sure what you mean."

"I think you do. I think you and he got to know each other when you were there. It would mean a great deal to me to hear what he's like. We really haven't had a chance to talk about that."

Lily's shoulders sagged with relief. It was foolish to think Eve could possibly know about the baby. Or that she'd even guess she and Cole had— "He's terribly handsome," she began, wanting to paint the picture just right. "But you know that. I see now, he's got your eyes."

Eve smiled as she leaned back in the big wing chair. "Go on."

"He's got himself a temper, that's true, but the men who work for him respect and admire him. He's a fair man who pushes for excellence, but he works harder than anyone else."

Lily took a sip of her tea, then she smiled. "He's also got a wicked sense of humor, although he doesn't particularly want people to think of him that way. In fact, he tries to hide a lot. His kindness, his tender side. He puts on a gruff, no-nonsense scowl and

thinks no one can see past it. But of course, everyone
who knows him any length of time does.''

"You did.''

"Yes, ma'am. I think I saw those traits that first
day. He tried to scare me away, but there was something more to it. A challenge. I wanted to spar with
him, and if I do say so myself, I gave as well as I
got.''

"I imagine you did.''

For a long moment, Lily's gaze went back to
Cole's ranch, to the stubborn son of a bitch who'd
stolen her heart. "He wasn't easy. Not ever. I think
it's because he's so afraid of being hurt. He'd be the
last one to admit it, but he cares so deeply about people, it makes him feel vulnerable. He was shattered
by Carrie and—''

"And?''

"And I didn't help any.'' She should stop. She was
telling Eve too much. But from the look in the older
woman's eyes, Lily could tell she wanted all of it.
The good and the bad. "I betrayed him, too, Eve, and
I've never been more sorry. I was a fool, and I took
all his old pain and made it fresh again. I wish I could
take it back.''

"So what you're saying to me is that he cared for
you.''

"Pardon?''

"You said it yourself.'' The old woman leaned forward again, a faint glimmer in her faded eyes. "It's
when he cares deeply that he can be hurt.''

"I suppose, but—''

"If I ask you a question, will you give me an honest answer?''

Lily wasn't sure she should say yes. But, heaven knew, lying had brought her to this sorry state. "Yes, ma'am."

"Are you in love with him?"

She closed her eyes for a moment and put her hand on her stomach. The second she realized what she'd done, she picked up her teacup, hoping the gesture wasn't noticed. Eve waited patiently as the old clock in the corner of the room counted out the seconds. "Yes, Eve. I'm in love with him." Tears welled again, which should have been impossible. But now she understood that there was a never-ending supply of tears. Enough for a lifetime. "I can't stop thinking about him. How I felt when I was with him. It was exciting, you know? My tummy got all quivery when I heard him walking down the hall. And when he touched me—" She stopped, afraid she'd said too much already.

"It's all right. I'm beyond being shocked. I figured you two had found the bedroom."

Lily felt her face heat. "It wasn't tawdry, Eve. It was—"

"Magic."

Lily froze as she heard the voice behind her. Low and deep, smooth as fine whiskey.

Eve smiled. "I believe you know my grandson."

Lily couldn't speak at all. She'd never wanted anything more in her life than this moment, and she was terrified if she said a word it would all disappear.

He walked across the carpet slowly, then moved in front of her. Her gaze traveled up his long, jean-clad legs to that big shiny belt, to the expanse of his chest and the blue-and-white western shirt he wore. She lingered on his hands. They held his hat nervously, moving round the rim. She'd saved the best for last, of course. She tilted her head up until their gazes met.

The thrill that coursed through her body was electric. He smiled at her, and that was all it took. She pushed herself out of her chair and the next second she was in his arms, and his hands were holding her tight, and his lips covered hers in fevered kisses.

"Lily," he whispered, then he kissed her some more. "It's been hell without you."

"I know," she said. "I haven't slept or been able to work. Cole, I'm so sorry. I've never been more sorry about anything in my life. I'd rather cut off my own arm than hurt you—"

He stopped her with his kiss, and she knew she'd been forgiven. But there was still one more thing to confess. One more truth to lay at his feet.

She pulled back and stepped away. "Cole, I—"

He shook his head. "Hold on, okay? Because I have a couple of things to say, and if I don't say them now, I might not have the nerve to say them later."

She nodded, noticing his hat on the floor. He'd dropped it when she'd jumped into his arms.

"I'm still not crazy about the fact that you lied to me. But I also know I would have shown you the door if you'd mentioned Eve. So, while I would have hoped for a different way, I can understand why you did what you did."

"Cole—"

He held up his hand. "I'm not through. I also did a lot of thinking about my family. About what I've been through, and what I've done with it. I'm proud of my ranch, but I don't love it. Not the way I should.

Not with the kind of passion that makes for a truly contented life. I've cut myself off from my past, and that includes all the good things, too. I've taken myself out of the game, and that's left me bitter and hard, and I won't do it anymore."

He stepped closer to her, so she could see the passion in his expression. "I'm giving up the ranch. Leasing it to Manny and Rita with an option to buy. I'm going to concentrate on my other business ventures. The things I do best." He turned around, looking at the far end of the room, where his grandmother stood, tears falling down her cheeks. "We've had ourselves some good talks," he said, his voice low and full of emotion. "Grandma has decided that I should take over the Texas Fund for Children. I've agreed. I'll be the new executive director."

Lily's heart thudded against her chest. Did that mean he'd be here? Live here in San Antonio?

His gaze came back to her. "I want to thank you for helping me see the truth. For pushing me up against that wall. If you hadn't, I would have kept my anger as my only companion. Probably for the rest of my life."

"Can I say something now?"

He shook his head. "Nope. Not quite. There's still one more thing I want to say." He took another step toward her and captured her trembling hands in his. "Lily, I've missed you. More than I ever dreamed I could miss another soul. I've missed that sassy mouth of yours. And your eyes, and the way you cock your right brow when you think I've said something stupid. In the past month, I've learned a lot about myself, but the one big truth, the fact that covers it all, is that I love you."

Now that he was giving her the chance to speak, she couldn't. She had such a lump in her throat and her heart was beating so fast and hard. She wanted to leap into his arms. To make this the perfect moment of her life. But she couldn't make her mouth work. No words would come out.

"Cole," Eve said, "I think Lily is trying to tell you something."

"You have any idea what it is?" He spoke as if she weren't right in front of him.

"Yes, I do. I think it has something to do with the night you two had a roll in the hay."

He looked at his grandmother, then back at her. The scowl she'd come to love was on his face and the look of confusion was in his eyes.

"She's right." Lily's voice sounded high and a little squeaky. "It does have to do with that night."

"What?"

"Well, remember that bandage on my hand? When I first got there?"

He nodded, his brows moving down another half inch. "So?"

"Well, see, I was taking antibiotics. For the dog bite. But what I didn't know was that, sometimes, certain antibiotics can reduce the efficacy of birth control pills."

"Pardon me?"

"I'm pregnant, Cole. I'm sorry. I only found out two days ago, and I left messages on your machine to call me. I was going to drive out to the ranch this weekend to tell you because I didn't want to keep any secrets from you.''

''You're pregnant?''

She nodded. ''We're pregnant.''

He blinked a few times, his face growing awfully pale. God, if he passed out, he'd take about ten Victorian dolls and an antique tea set with him.

''You want to sit down?''

He ignored the offer. ''We're pregnant? Are you sure?''

She nodded. ''I've been to the doctor. He says we're due in eight months.''

Cole seemed a bit wobbly, but he made it to the couch. He sat down and put his elbows on his knees. He stared at the floor for a long time.

Lily grew a bit concerned, and evidently so did Eve, because she came over to where Lily stood.

''Cole?''

He didn't acknowledge his grandmother at all.

''Cole, do I need to call you a doctor?''

That got him to look up. ''No, ma'am.'' He stood and took a step toward Eve. He grasped her small shoulders in his large hands and kissed her on the cheek. ''You're gonna be a great-grandma,'' he said.

''Isn't that something.''

Cole just stood there while a dopey grin overtook his face. Lily could see the child he'd once been. ''It sure as hell is.''

''Will you do something for me, son?''

''Anything.''

''Ask the woman to marry you before she faints.''

Cole blinked. Then laughed. He kissed Eve again, then let her go. He approached Lily slowly, still smiling like the cat who ate the canary. "You need to know something."

"What?"

"I was gonna do this before you told me."

"Do what?"

He took her in his arms and kissed her hard. "Ask you to be mine."

"Your what?" She had to hear it from his lips before she would believe it. "Surrogate mother? Wife in name only?"

"God, no." He squeezed her tighter. "I want you to be my wife. My companion. The mother of our children. I love you, Lily, and I want to grow old by your side. So, will you?"

She kissed him, and the tears from her cheeks made him all wet. "Yes, yes, yes. I will. I love you forever, and I'll bear your children, and I'll give you hell when you need it. But no matter what, I'll love you. Absolutely. With all my heart."

"Then it's settled."

She nodded.

His gaze on hers grew very serious. "You woke me up, Lily. You taught me how to feel again. How to love. And I'm grateful to you."

She smiled. And then she kissed him. And she knew, in that way she had, that this was the best thing she'd ever done. And that they would be together for the rest of their lives. They'd have a houseful of children, and laughter and joy and pain and everything else that came when two people joined together in marriage. She saw her future, and it was in his arms. Her intuition was never wrong.

TRUEBLOOD, TEXAS *continues*
next month with
HIS BROTHER'S FIANCÉE
By Jasmine Cresswell

*Emily Sutton is up to her ears in the final plans
for her lavish society wedding when her fiancé
informs her that he can't marry her. So she
assumes Jordan Chambers, her fiancé's black
sheep brother, is offering to save her from
the embarrassment of being publicly jilted in
order to salvage an important business merger
between their families. But Jordan's not
motivated by family at all. What he's always
wanted is Emily, and he's not about to
squander his only chance.*

Here's a preview!

"I THOUGHT IT might be a good idea if we got married tomorrow." Jordan made the suggestion with a casualness that would have been entirely appropriate if he'd been suggesting that she might like to try out a new recipe for brunch on Sunday.

Emily clutched the back of the nearest chair. *Jordan had asked her to marry him.* She was quite sure she'd heard that. Unless she was hallucinating. Was she? She felt her mouth start to drop open again, and she hurriedly closed it.

The study was not a good place to be alone with a Chambers male, she decided. First Michael had called off their wedding for no reason at all. Now Jordan was suggesting something even more totally crazy. So crazy, in fact, that Emily felt a spurt of genuine alarm. She hadn't been serious in suggesting Jordan and Michael were suffering from the onset of insanity. Maybe she should have been.

"I don't think marriage would work out too well for us," she said, trying to keep her voice soft and nonthreatening. She even managed a small, reassuring smile. When dealing with lunatics, it was best to be gentle. "Thanks for asking, Jordan, but if you remember, we don't like each other. I have this quaint, old-fashioned dislike of men who sleep with other men's wives."

Jordan might have lost his mind, but his vision remained acute, and his physical coordination excellent. In three quick strides, he crossed the room and pulled her away from the door, spread-eagling his body between her and her escape route.

"Sorry," he said, sounding sincerely apologetic as he pocketed the key. "But I really need you to listen to my proposal."

"I already had one of those from Michael," she replied tightly. "I believe I'm a little burned out on proposals from the Chambers men."

His gaze narrowed. "*Proposition* might be a better word in my case. I'm offering a face-saving deal, Emily. You owe it to yourself to listen. Marry me tomorrow, and the joint business venture between my father and yours can go on as planned. Marry me tomorrow, and the ceremony will probably be over before half the guests even notice that you're exchanging rings with the wrong brother—"

"Thanks again for the generous offer, Jordan, but before we get carried away, let's remember there's one teensy-tiny problem with your scheme."

"What's that?"

"Half the guests might not notice that I'd married the wrong brother, but I would." Emily spoke more harshly than she'd intended, mostly because for a few insane seconds, she'd actually found herself considering his proposition. She was surely hitting a new low to contemplate accepting Jordan's proposal just because it would provide a groom for tomorrow's ceremony.

Jordan shrugged. "It wouldn't be a lifetime sentence," he said. "We can have the big, splashy wedding our parents planned, and then, in a few months, we can get a quiet, civilized divorce.''

"Divorce is never civilized," Emily said. "It's a heartbreaking betrayal of promises."

HARLEQUIN®
Makes any time special®

If you've enjoyed getting to know
the Garrett family, Harlequin® invites you
to come back and visit the Finders Keepers agency!
Just collect three (3) proofs of purchase from the
back pages of three (3) different Trueblood, Texas
titles and receive a free Trueblood, Texas book
that's not available in retail outlets!

Just complete the order form and send it, along with three (3)
proofs of purchase from three (3) different Trueblood, Texas
titles, to: TRUEBLOOD, TEXAS, P.O. Box 9047, Buffalo, NY
14269-9047 or P.O. Box 613, Fort Erie, Ontario L2A 5X3.

Name: _____

Address: _____ City: _____

State/Prov.: _____ Zip/Postal Code: _____

Account Number: __ __ __ __ __ __ __ __ __ __ __ __

Please specify which title(s) you would like to receive:

☐ 0-373-65090-6   **Hero for Hire** by Jill Shalvis
☐ 0-373-65091-4   **Her Protector** by Liz Ireland
☐ 0-373-65092-2   **Lover Under Cover** by Charlotte Douglas
☐ 0-373-65093-0   **A Family at Last** by Debbi Rawlins

Remember——for each title selected, you must send three (3) original proofs of purchase!

(Please allow 4-6 weeks for delivery. Offer expires October 31, 2002.)
(The below proof of purchase should be cut off the ad)

093 KIT DAFL   PHTBTPOP

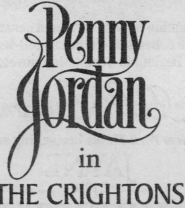

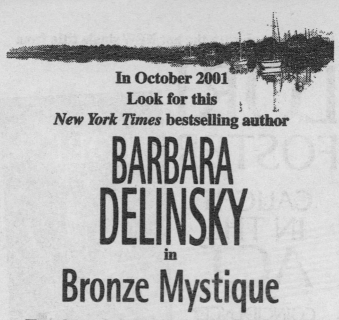

Get *caught* up with the hot NEW single title from

LORI FOSTER

CAUGHT IN THE ACT

COINCIDENCE?
Not.

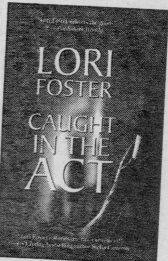

Mick Dawson, undercover cop. He's got his hands full with a pushy broad who claims she's just in the wrong place at the wrong time. Except all the perps seem to know everything there is to know about her. Who're you going to believe? Only one way to find out. Get *really* close.

Lela DeBraye (aka Delta Piper), mystery writer. She's as confused as he is, but mostly because he's got the sweetest smile, when he smiles. Still, he's sticking with her twenty-four/seven—is this love or duty? Is he her protector or her captor?

Look for *CAUGHT IN THE ACT* in September 2001.